Hands Across the Moon

Hands across the

MOON

jane g. meyer

thirsty(?)™ an imprint of
tyndale house
publishers

Visit Tyndale's exciting Web site at www.thirstybooks.com

Thirsty(?) is a trademark of Tyndale House Publishers, Inc.

Edited by Lorie Popp

Designed by Beth Sparkman

Published in association with the literary agency of Janet Kobobel Grant, Books & Such, 4788 Carissa Ave., Santa Rosa, CA 95405.

Scripture quotations are taken from the *Holy Bible,* New Living Translation, copyright © 1996. Used by permission of Tyndale House Publishers, Inc., Wheaton, Illinois 60189. All rights reserved.

Library of Congress Cataloging-in-Publication Data

Meyer, Jane G.
    Hands across the moon / Jane G. Meyer.
        p. cm.
Summary: Gretchen and Mia, best friends and juniors in high school, are separated when Gretchen's family moves from California to Ecuador but continue to share their hearts and experiences through their letters.
    ISBN 0-8423-8286-0 (pbk.)
[1. Best friends—Fiction. 2. Friendship—Fiction. 3. Letters—Fiction. 4. Christian life—Fiction. 5. Interpersonal relations—Fiction. 6. Ecuador—Fiction.] I. Title.
    PZ7.M5716 Han 2003
    [Fic]—dc21   2003000208

Printed in the United States of America

07 06 05 04 03
7   6   5   4   3   2   1

To Kristin, who told me stories of faraway places
and trusted me with her heart.

To Carol, who stayed behind and
will always remain my dearest friend.

And to God above, who blesses us with others
to love and learn by. . . .

Many thanks
to my Douglas . . .
and to Abbey Hardy,
Mary Timby, and
Annie Bennington,
who loved and played
with the little ones
while I wrote.

Summer

June 14
Quito, Ecuador

★ ★ ★

Dear Mia,

I am hopeless. I told you I would give this move a chance. I promised I would keep my chin up, stay positive, and be patient. Enough of patience. Enough of promises. I'm fed up with this place. It's dirty, it's gross, we have no home, I have no clothes, and I stand out like a giant in a sea of mini-people.

How could I be dragged away from all my friends and smile about it? Am I supposed to just trot off to some humid, bug-infested, Spanish-speaking country, where everywhere you look there's a volcano waiting to erupt, and say, "Thanks, Mom. Thanks, Dad. This is exactly what I had envisioned for my junior year of high school!" Good grief, six months ago I thought Ecuador was a country in Africa!

At least I have an easy out. I'm blaming all of my problems—past, present, and future—on my dad. He's the one who said yes to the university. And I used to think he

was an intelligent professor. . . . Now when I look at him
I want to growl. I hate it here!

Thanks for helping me pack. I'm sure you didn't want
to be doing anything else, ha-ha. Bringing my journal
along was the best idea you've had in ages—not that you're
not always full of bright ideas. This journal's the only
friend I have anymore. Unfortunately, the first few
pages, where you wrote the poem, got a little soaked on
the plane. Okay, I admit it—I was crying. But I just
had to read your words one last time before we
took off.

What a scene I made on that plane. I sat frozen in my
window seat, trapped between the glass and a squealing
Elsie. I sobbed as I was forced to fly south, like some silly
bird. My hands were shaking, and tears dripped everywhere.
It took two days for the journal to dry out, and it's taken
even longer for my swollen face to recover from the
trauma.

"Come on, Gretchen, look for the good," I hear you
saying. "Find the bright spot. You can do it." You're right.
I need to stop blabbering, but I refuse.

Quito stinks. (KEETOW STEENKS.) It's a big
city—confusing—oh, and did I already say dirty? You

know how I love dirt. My dad sure had me fooled with all those romantic images about Ecuador he painted in my head.

"Where's the beauty?" I ask him. "Do you mean that incredibly beautiful orchid growing on the old, dilapidated cement wall covered with barbed wire? Or are you talking about the church made from pure gold where all the begging children pick your pockets?" The contrast of good and bad, the ugly mixed into the beautiful, is shocking. This city is one giant mess of opposites.

So aren't you happy I wrote? I'm such a fountain of overflowing exclamations!

Oh, and before I sign off, we're staying with the Johnsons while our house is being disinfected. Yes, you read right. He's that professor-friend of my dad's who studies anything that slithers. Remember when he stayed at our home last summer and my mom found out he had a snake in his suitcase? And the worst thing is, Shannon Johnson loves Ecuador, which makes her hard to take. She's stuck-up, dresses just like an East Coast sorority girl, and to top it off, her gorgeous brothers are away in the States for the summer. Just my luck. She makes me squirm when she talks about the jungle . . . and malaria . . . and diarrhea . . . like they're some fun facts of life.

I just peeked out the window and it's raining again. Whoever heard of rain in June? Ugh.

I miss you, Mia. Write soon. Come and save me if you can.

Love,
Gretchen

June 24
Pacific Palisades, California

Dear Gretchen,

They must have sent your letter by bicycle instead of by air. It seems like I've been waiting for weeks to hear from you! I got your note this morning, and like I promised, I'm writing immediately.

First of all, please don't call yourself hopeless. Maybe you were just having a bad day. . . . No, I can tell it was more than a bad day. I'm sorry, Gretchen. Try to be positive about the move. Who knows what God has in store for you? Just think about your beautiful smile, your generous heart, your bright blue eyes, and how much better it feels to spread beauty and goodness.

Anyway, I'm sorry to hear about the dirt and the bugs and the rain and the flight and the Johnsons. It all sounds awful. How does your mom feel? And your sisters?

I hate to think of your crying on that plane. It's

not the same without you here—not at church, not at the beach—not the same anywhere. I'll think of an escape plan to get you home.

Camp was fun, but it doesn't seem right to tell you about it now. Our old friend Steve got into trouble, as usual, and I behaved, as always.

Chin up. I miss you more than you know.

Much love,
Mia

P.S. Have your clothes come yet?

June 30
Quito, Ecuador

★ ★ ★

Dear Mia,

I'm still in a funk. Maybe I'll come out of it by
college.

I've been shuttled to another planet—I'm certain of it now.
When I go for a walk here in **KEETOW**, I feel like there's
an enormous sign flashing above my head that says
"Gringo, Gringo. Come and Stare for 50 Cents!" The first
time our whole family went out together we looked like a
troop of giant Vikings marching in to take over the town. No
more of that family stuff. I'm boycotting all family outings.

Time for your scolding. It was totally unfair of you to
write such a short letter. I don't care how insensitive it
seemed to you to write about camp or whatever . . . I need
good news, bad news, any news, just more news to distract
me from this nightmare of a move. So get writing . . . and
write long. Tell me all about Steve. Tell me about camp. Tell
me about anything. I'm counting on you.

We're moving into our house on Monday. It's about time.

I need my own room! Good riddance to Shannon Johnson, though she has gotten a bit nicer with time. And she has a car.

No, no sign of my clothes. Worse, my mom and dad and sisters all love it here. Have you come up with an escape plan yet? I could hike north, you could hike south, and we could meet in the middle.

Love,
Wretched Gretchen

July 7
Pacific Palisades, California

Dear Gretchen,

Here goes my attempt at a long letter. I hope my words help you feel even a little happier.

Summer is going well and camp was fun. Of course, it would have been so much better if you had been there. As usual, Steve, with his new batch of camp admirers, entertained us and was constantly in trouble. I don't know how, but he always manages to wiggle out of any real punishment. One night we played a new game. He slipped off into the dark with a new girl from Southcoast Church and was later found, past curfew, squeezed into a corner of the cafeteria with her. Somehow, instead of having to memorize the Gospel of John or do a thousand push-ups like the counselors threatened, Steve talked them into letting him help in the cafeteria during breakfast. He looked very cute in his white apron.

Now that I'm back home, I'm also back at the gym. The coaches always frown and shake their fingers at me when I take a week off. I'm not sure what they think will happen. Maybe I'll gain 20 pounds or forget how to do a cartwheel? They're awfully protective. But I enjoy the summer workouts. Not just because of a week off now and then, but because I get to try out the new tricks I've been dreaming about all year.

Besides gymnastics, I've been down to the beach on and off. Yesterday I drove to Carol's house, and five of us met to go sailing on Stuart's Hobie Cat. (It wasn't the same without you!) We all took turns sailing. When I got on board the winds picked up, and we tacked the boat around. I stumbled over something, hit my head on the mast, and we capsized. Leave it to me to throw us all overboard! I have a big bump on my head, but it's no worse than the normal bruises I get at the gym every day.

Please tell me more about Ecuador. When I read words like <u>volcano, orchid, gringo, jungle, gold,</u> I want to know more. I want to see those things too.

I hope you've moved into your new house by now

and are all settled with your things. I know how you love your space. Especially a place where you can read and write in your journal. Will school start for you soon? Is it still raining? I'm still working on an escape plan. . . .

Please forgive me for sending you a short letter last time. I know this letter isn't pages and pages, but I'm being "summoned" by Charlie the Tuna. We're riding our bikes to Mom's shop, where she expects us to dust and mop and greet customers with a smile until closing.

I miss you too. Best friends always.

Love,
Mia

July 18
Quito, Ecuador

★ ★ ★

Dear Mia,

Thanks for the longish letter. I liked hearing about gym and camp. I forgive you for not writing more, because you're my best friend, my only friend, a busy friend, and . . . maybe with a little practice you can be a more long-winded friend.

Me, me, me . . . leave it to me to attract tragedy. You won't believe what happened! I still don't.

Two weeks ago there was a huge storm out in the middle of the Pacific Ocean. We didn't hear a word of it because it fizzled long before hitting land. Yesterday my dad, who I still consider wacky for bringing us all here, got a call from a ship's officer. The officer said he was phoning from Guayaquil, a port city in southern Ecuador. "Bad news," the man said.

Our boat sank. The boat that was happily floating along, carrying all of our things from California, sank! Can you believe it? All of our stuff—I mean ALL of our stuff—SANK! Sank, sank, sank to the bottom of the ocean!

"The authorities" are full of conflicting stories. Suppos-edly the navigators misjudged the direction of the storm, and once they were being tossed about like rag dolls, there was no way out.

Then, just like in a fairy tale, the boat ran into an unin-habited island, where a coral reef set to work smashing it up. They mentioned something about turtles, but I didn't quite get it all. I don't think the turtles saved the crew or anything, but I know everyone got to shore alive.

People were sent from Costa Rica to check out the damage to the boat, which is almost totally submerged and laying on its side. They say our crates are still on board and that they'll contact us when they get the boat towed to shore.

UNBELIEVABLE!

It will be months before we see any of our stuff in those crates. By then everything will be sprouting with seaweed and little crabs, and sea anemones will be living in my beau-tiful Toscana shoes that I bought with my own money!

I have to admit I was wimpy about the whole ordeal and cried buckets when I first heard the news. But that's done with now. I haven't gone as far as my parents have, though. They laughed (I told you my dad needs help) and said, "We're in God's hands, and who needs stuff, anyway?"

So all this sinking news doesn't leave much strength in my hand to write more. I'll be quick about a few things and then write again later.

We are in our house, but now I have zilch to put in my new room. No reminders of my old life. Nothing to put on except these same dirty socks! I've got to tell you about the guards, guns, maid, and cook. But not now. Send me a picture of yourself, will you? Or if you took some snapshots at camp of Steve and his sweetheart huddled in the cafeteria, send those.

Love your dirty-footed friend,
Gretchen

July 20
Quito, Ecuador

★ ★ ★

Hey, Mimi,

My hand is well rested, and I'm writing again. I've gotten off the sinking-ship subject. It's amazing what a chocolate bar can do for one's mood, and sitting here now after just gulping one down makes me living proof.

THE HOUSE.

We just moved in. I like Shannon Johnson more now that we're not stepping on each other's bras and underwear. I suppose she had a lot to put up with, seeing as she's not used to having us four sisters bombard her bathroom and chatter at her constantly. And she did zoom Karen and me around in the afternoons in her little Chevy-Suzuki something. Everything is a Chevy here, whether it's remotely related to a Chevrolet or not. Well, they don't say Chevy-Mercedes, but there are Chevy-Isuzus and Chevy LUVs. . . . They have a real fetish for Chevys!

Shannon drives like a maniac, and I thought every time I got in with her that we would get splattered on the pavement. But we didn't, and she showed us some fun places to go.

Back to the house.

Shannon said the area we live in is pretty safe. It's called Quicentro and is smack-dab in the middle of town. Now don't think our neighborhood is like one you'd see at home with manicured lawns and tall stately trees. . . . No. The streets here are narrow, and yards in front of homes do not exist. Instead they have huge walls and gates that surround every residence. Most of these walls and gates have spikes on top of them. Maybe that's what makes the neighborhood so safe! The homes are made from cement. Some are white plaster like ours, some are elegant, and some look like ugly cement blocks.

Around our house is a whole assortment of little shops and houses. There's even a dirt patch nearby, which they call a park. Dirt or not, kids use it constantly, usually to play soccer. Dogs also use it. Right now it's a mud puddle.

Because it takes at least 10 minutes just to fiddle with all the different keys to the gates and doors to the house, my parents are trying to think of ways to simplify the process. I'm serious. I have four keys: one for the outside gate, one for the inside gate, one for the small gate into the front courtyard, and one for the front door. I'm all for a magic wardrobe, like little Lucy found in Narnia.

The house is built in the shape of a square. In the middle of the square is an outdoor courtyard. Half of the courtyard is like a mini-backyard with a tree, some flowers, which are flooded from the rain, and a bit of grass. They say the weather is so nice here that we'll be able to use the courtyard all year long. At least when it's not raining . . . like it is now.

The inside of the house is not very strange. It is a two-story, and all of the bedrooms are on the second floor. Karen and I are sharing a room, as are the munchkins, Elsie and Susanna. I've already set up all the rules for my room, and I'm sure with a little arm-twisting, Karen will be a good roommate. She's so quiet and I'm so loud—I think I have the better end of the deal this time.

Not only are we renting the house, but we're renting the furniture. That's kind of weird, but because my room is so great, I don't mind. My bed is definitely the most interesting piece of furniture in the house. It has a hand-carved headboard made of black wood that smells of coconuts mixed with coffee. Carved in the center of the wood are small tropical birds, and around the edges and along the sides of the bed are more carvings of trees and branches with little nests and birds hiding in them.

Karen's bed is similar, except hers has carvings of orchids, vines, and butterflies. We also have an enormous wooden cabinet where we will put our clothes, if we ever get any! Then there's a little chair with a green embroidered seat that sits next to our balcony.

Oh, the balcony! We have two tall French doors that open onto a balcony. It's really too small to be used for much, but I love it. Every morning and evening I go out there to brush my hair in the open air. It looks out over the courtyard, and there are two other balconies in the house just like it—one in my parents' room and one in Elsie and Susanna's room. I keep the doors open all the time to let the breeze come in.

Now for the play I'm writing. Romeo comes and visits me. He sings Spanish love songs to me from the courtyard and recites poetry that weakens my knees. I sit on the little chair with the green embroidered seat and listen to his music with my eyes closed and my golden hair blowing in the wind. I wear a white flowing nightgown made from the finest silk, and he begs me to jump down to him. Play over.

But more shocking than Romeo is the fact that we have a

maid and a cook! Shannon said it's normal for anyone living in this part of town to have house help, and now I know why my mom was so excited to try living in Ecuador for a while. It's good news for the family, because now we get to eat real food, like rice, instead of stuff out of boxes and cans. Mom seems happy and has started painting again.

Our maid's name is Stella, and her room is downstairs. She must be about 20 years old, is super quiet and shy, and has the most enchanting smile. Her skin is dark and perfect, and her eyes are so big, I can't believe some Ecuadorian prince hasn't swept her off to his castle. Her hair hangs down her back in one long braid, and she smiles at me and lowers her eyes whenever I pass her in the house.

She speaks only Spanish, so I haven't talked with her much, but I hope I can soon, once I get to school and start learning a bit. I want to know all of her beauty secrets: like what creams she uses on her face to make it so smooth and how she gets her hair to shine in every light. I also want to know where her handsome prince is hiding.

Stella stays busy all day, even coming in to straighten my shoes and make my bed, which I always leave in a heap. It's weird. My mom says it's okay if she cleans up a little after us, but—you can hear it coming, can't you? "You

girls better not get used to it because it won't last forever."
It's a mom's job to say stuff like that.

Our cook comes in the morning and leaves right after lunch, which we eat at exactly 2:30 in the afternoon. Her name is Juana, but my mom told us to call her señora. It's hard to guess how old she is—maybe 40? maybe 60? She always sings or hums when she cooks. Always. Except for when she's chasing me out of the kitchen with a spoon waving dangerously close to my backside. She has yet to wallop me on the behind when I'm sneaking bites of this or that out of her pans, but I'm sure she'll get me one of these days. I like her.

When Juana comes in the morning, she carries the same straw basket overstuffed with vegetables and meats. Since she leaves after lunch, she makes something simple for us—like soup—to heat up for dinner. We eat rice every day with every meal. We learned quickly that we better eat up when food is on the table because there's no place to store leftovers. We do have a refrigerator, but it's this little metal box, barely cold enough to keep milk in. Anyway, life is pretty different than back home. No more Cheerios or Chee·tos.

Oh yeah, I forgot to mention the guards. They're all over town, in front of buildings, banks, grocery stores, and some even patrol our neighborhood. Most of them are young guys in uniforms, holding huge guns. I haven't the faintest clue as to what their real purpose is, and I'm not sure whether to trust them or stick my tongue out at them.

Besides the guns, the guards also have whistles that they use to call for help. At least that's what I think they are for. So far, I have only heard the other kind of whistle, the whit-whoo kind. They call to me and other girls when we walk by. They get pretty creative with their whistle tunes, and sometimes I end up laughing so hard I have to sit down and wait for them to stop.

They call me names too, but right now I only recognize the word gringo. I must hear that one on every corner! It's like walking through a construction zone each time I leave the house. You know me. I don't get intimidated easily, and some of the guards are cute in their own way, with their funny little caps perched on their heads. Maybe when I can speak Spanish they will seem more like people and less like birds tweeting out love songs.

Speaking of not being able to speak . . . I wish I spoke Spanish. I'm sure if my parents had known that we'd be whisked off to Ecuador someday, they would have had us studying Spanish on weekends and holidays even. Four years of French aren't getting me anywhere, except confused.

They say it'll be the hardest for me to learn since I'm the oldest. I can see that Elsie and Susanna, who are now 6½ and 8¾, are already picking up words and phrases that somehow pass right by me.

School should help. Classes begin the first week of October. That's a whole different story, though, that I'll write about later. Being summer still, it's too painful right now to think about school.

Make an announcement at church that I want letters—lots of them. I want to know all of the news (especially the "who's dating who" news)! So, without further ado, as Romeo would say, I need to end this handwritten work of art and get it to my dad, who is slowly becoming less crazy. He's going to the post office now and then to the authorities to get news on our sunken boat! He's calling for me.

Mucho love,
Gretchen

July 29
Pacific Palisades, California

Dear Gretchen,

I can't believe your boat sank! I feel so bad for you—that you have lost all your things. If there is anything I can send or anything of mine that you want, just tell me. I'm not sure what you need, but I would be happy to give you ANYTHING.

I got both of your letters, one after the other. I was shocked to hear about the boat, but I had fun reading about Romeo and your balcony. Your life is so exciting! Maybe Ecuador has more to offer you than you thought! Maybe someday you'll thank your dad for taking you down there, instead of calling him crazy. You did get one detail confused in your Romeo story, though. And I know because I helped you pack. You don't own a long flowing nightgown. All you have is that Tweety bird nightshirt that someone gave you ages ago!

So what will you do about clothes? And your

parents and all their books and other belongings? What will happen? I'm worried. Please let me know what I can do. I could have a car wash and raise some money . . . or do a thousand cartwheels for a dollar a turn . . . have my parents talk to their friends. . . . Just let me know what you think and need.

Everything is fine here . . . sort of. Monique and I went down to Redondo Beach the other Saturday to watch Steve and Marco play in a two-man volleyball tournament. They did fairly well but were knocked out in the quarterfinals by a team from Santa Monica. Once they had finished their last match we caught up with them, and the four of us sat around in the sand for a while, just talking. It was too hot to talk for long though, so we ran for the water.

The waves were a bit unpredictable because of an offshore storm. Monique and I were floating around while Steve and Marco swam out to the half-mile marker. After I played in the waves a bit, I noticed a big swell coming at me. I was caught, with no time to get out or duck under. The first wave of the swell crashed on top of me, and I struggled to keep my feet on the bottom, but the white water was more than I could handle and tugged me under. I tried to get deeper, away from the turbulence, but I couldn't. Then I was pulled to the bottom, like being sucked down a drain, and pushed into the sand. I came up spitting, and of course, another wave caught me and another and another. . . .

Then IT happened.

I was rescued by the lifeguard!

I can't tell you how embarrassed I was. I'm sure you're laughing now as you imagine me being towed in by that little red buoy. The lifeguard had a good grip on me as she pulled me backward through the waves. I kept saying, "I'm all right. I can manage from here." But she was thorough! She dragged me halfway across the beach, and I finally escaped after five minutes of questioning. A crowd gathered to "make sure I was okay." Monique had been lucky and saw the swell in time. She waited out the big waves in the deeper water and swam in after the swell passed.

Soon Marco and Steve came to shore, and they

had to hear the story three times straight. I've never seen two boys laugh so hard in my life! They were rolling in the sand saying, "You're killin' me . . . the lifeguard . . . ? the buoy . . . ?"

That night I took a shower before I went to bed. When I woke up in the morning I found sand buried so deep in my eyebrows and hair that I think some must be lodged in my brain too. Don't be surprised if this letter comes sprinkled with sand and smelling like sea salt!

Wow! You have a maid, a cook, and guards? How I would love to come and visit someday. Have you met anyone yet? Anyone our age? What about at the church your dad told you about before you left? Any boys?

You know, I think you are the luckiest girl on earth. Just think of all the experiences you'll have. The jungle, a new language, Latin boyfriends! I do wish you were here so we could finish high school together, but God must have great things in store for you! Not like me, plodding along the same boring path—going to the gym, going to school, going to church. Always the same old thing.

Well, now I'm getting depressing, and my boat didn't even sink! I'll close for now until I can come up with more interesting things to say. Say hello to Karen, whose blonde hair grows faster than seaweed. Tell Elsie that I don't have anyone to play tag with anymore and Susanna that I miss her climbing up in my lap and reading stories together.

And don't forget your parents, who always try to feed me whenever I visit. I miss that.

I'll write again soon. Best Friends Forever.

Love,
Mia

August 6
Quito, Ecuador

★ ★ ★

My Dear Sandy One,

The lifeguard really used that red buoy to pull you in? Well, that must have been a "character building" experience for you! Not that you need any more character. You've got more than anyone I know.

You may not be the smartest wave rider, but you are definitely the best of friends! Yesterday I received a sweet letter from you, and today I received THE BOX.

THE BOX is huge. My sisters and I cried when we saw all of the goodies inside. We feel so loved by everyone at church and especially by your family, who obviously organized the whole thing. We haven't looked through it carefully yet, but there must be enough clothes and other items for three families to use. You are sneaky but wonderful.

Thanks especially for the gift you sent just for me. The wrapping said "Open in secret," so I snuck into my room and unwrapped everything alone on my bed. The first few things that tumbled out were the Chee•tos and the new socks. I gobbled up one pack of the Chee•tos right away and put on the new socks. They looked so clean! Next I opened the gift wrapped in tissue. I can't tell you how I laughed! A white, flowing nightgown, perfect for those nights when I hear Romeo throwing imaginary stones at my balcony door! It really is beautiful and a big change from Tweety bird.

The fourth gift left my mouth hanging open. I know your mother, the weaver, was definitely involved. If you weren't my best friend, and if we didn't spend so much time in your room as kids, I would have thought you sent me your cross. But this one is different, even if only slightly. I love it. It's like having a portion of a queen's treasure. I feel like a princess. I'm going to hang it over my bed, the same way you have yours in your room.

I showed the gifts to my mom this afternoon and she was speechless. She hugged me as she left the room and said, "The Lord always has a better plan, doesn't he?" I agree.

Next week we're off to the jungle. I can't wait to leave the city behind for a few days, but I'm more than nervous about the packing list: extra-strength bug spray, rubber boots, rain poncho, flashlights, antiseptic, malaria pills. . . . Can you imagine me stomping around in rubber boots? Not showering for a week and smelling like antiseptic aren't my idea of fun.

After we get back, we've planned one more vacation before school starts in October. My dad says we should travel and explore as much as possible since we're here. Too bad he doesn't think traveling is soaking up sun on an isolated beach.

I still can't believe what you all sent us. Please give your mom a gigantic kiss from me, and tell her I love the cross. Well, I'll write her myself, but you tell her too. And thank you for the Chee•tos and the socks and the nightgown. You know me too well.

Best friends forever.

Love,
Princess Gretchen

P.S. There's a guard down the street . . . Javier. He is the only one who doesn't make a fool of himself when I walk by. I wish my Spanish were better!

August 16
Pacific Palisades, California

Dear Princess Gretchen!

I'm at my mom's shop and it's quiet today, so I thought I'd write. How are you? I'm glad you liked the box. We had such fun putting it together.

I suppose by now you've been to the jungle and back. The only jungle I see is here in the shop, where skeins of yarn are hanging from the ceiling and piled all over the floor. Yarn isn't the only thing that makes it seem like a jungle in here. Between the spiders, moths, and cockroaches, the shop's got the animal kingdom covered. There might even be a few exotic, never-before-discovered creatures lurking in the corners of this old place. You'll have to tell me what kind of creatures you found lurking in the real jungles of Ecuador.

Mom's stocking up for fall. Once the cool weather comes, people start thinking about knitting blankets, sweaters, and warm woolly socks. It's her busiest time of year. I told her I would help out when I have time. But once school begins, time is one thing I won't have much of.

It's amazing how I can write and not say anything! Maybe it's because there's not much to say. I miss you. The beach is still here. Everyone is just the same except Steve, who traded his beautiful brown curls for a buzz cut, and is now dating Adriana. She must be his fourth girlfriend this year.

Do you think maybe I have a secret crush on Steve? I know we've all been friends for a long time—growing up together in church. I was even his "line buddy" in kindergarten and got to hold his hand every day when we walked out to the playground. But I seem to think about him more than other boys. I just love how he looks straight into you with those big brown eyes when you're talking to him, and there's always a smile and a funny word to follow. Anyway, I know he would never ask me out. I'm too busy and too . . . quiet. And I'm . . . just a friend.

Gymnastics is great, but the coaches need a vacation. They're too protective of me and try to hold me back. They think I'm made of glass. As if their future, not mine, could be ruined by a bad landing.

Speaking of landings, my ankles are holding up. My goal is to make it through this season without an injury. I'm conservative sometimes, but if I always hold back, I won't be ready for competition. I pray at times that the coaches would leave the decisions to me. (Wishful prayers.)

Right now I feel confident and strong. I know doors are opening for me. College is taken care of, my coaches say, if I just stay healthy. Any college. But now my goal is to win nationals, not think about college. There's plenty of time to think about that later.

Enough of gymnastics. It's not like I don't live and breathe the sport.

Summer is passing quickly. Yikes! I wish I had until October to start school like you do. Uh-oh, in comes a customer. She looks like she walked right out of the '60s. Long braids, woven coat, and she's smoking a cigar! Good grief, she must not have seen the sign on the door!

I'll write again soon. Best friends forever and ever.

Love,
Mia

August 22
Quito, Ecuador

Mia,

I've been grounded for days, and I'm so bored! I hate this city. I hate not having friends. I hate having to always be with my sisters. They are driving me crazy! That's why I'm grounded. Karen and I have been in more catfights this week than in the last five years combined.

A few days ago, the two of us went down the street to get something at the store. We started to fight about clothes on the way back because she was wearing a shirt that we agreed would be mine. She didn't even ask me if she could wear it and took it anyway. I didn't notice right away, but when I realized she had it on, I blew up. I screamed at her, ran home, and locked her out of the front gate. She didn't have any keys. My parents were away, and I wouldn't let Stella open the front door.

My mom said I was being childish. Dangerous even. But I think no one respects me. Karen takes my things without asking, my parents are always making me baby-sit, and

Susanna and Elsie won't listen to me. Shouldn't I have a life too? My parents grounded me for a week, so all I do is sit here and brood. Ugh. This family is so maddening! This country is so maddening!

I won't get anywhere with this letter. I shouldn't even mail it. Send someone to rescue me. Someone who won't drown me in lectures.

Gretchen

September 2
Pacific Palisades, California

Dear Gretchen,

What's wrong? Your sisters have never bothered you that much, have they? I was always amazed at how well you all got along. I don't blame you for being mad at Karen, but . . . I guess she shouldn't take your things without asking.

You didn't tell me anything about your trip to the jungle. Did you go? Or did you have to cancel it for some reason? I wanted to hear all about the mist and the canopy and the jaguars camouflaged in the trees. . . . I hope you're okay. That you were just having a bad day. Please write again and tell me that you and Karen are trying to work things out.

My mom wanted me to tell you how much she appreciated the thank-you note you sent. She loved making the cross and feels like you are one of her daughters too. I think she misses you as much as I do.

I've been down myself lately. School begins

tomorrow, and there's so much pressure on me to do well in everything. Things at the gym are far from wonderful, mostly because Jamie won't speak to me. We've been friends for so long, and now she says I'm full of myself and stuck-up. I cried. Am I, Gretchen? Am I full of myself? I've been trying so hard not to be. Sometimes it's hard to be better at something than your friends are.

Jamie thinks I don't understand, but I do. Her body is changing, and I feel bad for her. In gymnastics, when your body matures, you need more strength, your center of gravity changes, and who knows what else happens. I'm sad for her—and for our friendship.

Last night I was reading Hinds' Feet on High Places. A certain passage made me think about forgiveness, about making good come out of bad experiences. It was great timing for me to read those words. So I've decided to forgive Jamie even if she is still upset with me. Please pray for me. I'm going to try my hardest to make up with her.

I hope I get a happier letter from you next time. It makes me miserable thinking that you hate it there. Only a few weeks ago you were so happy the way you wrote about your room and your balcony and Romeo.

I'm sorry I have to go. I needed to be at the gym 10 minutes ago.

Much love,
Mia

September 16
Quito, Ecuador

★ ★ ★

Dear Mia,

I hardly know where to begin. I've wanted to write this letter for weeks, but I couldn't think of how to tell you the truth about my life without sending you into shock. I still haven't figured out what to say. Except that I am a fool.

Before I say anything, swear on the Holy Bible that you won't tell a soul. Swear it! I feel so gross about what has happened, I would never EVER come back to California if anyone found out. I'd hate you.

The day before we went to the jungle and before I started fighting with my sisters, I was walking back to our house after running an errand for Mom. There's a corner store a few blocks away, and she'd asked me to buy some batteries. It was so hot, and I was tired, crabby, and not watching. Not thinking! A dumb song was stuck in my head, and I was counting the cracks in the cement walls. Oh, Mia, it was horrible. It makes me sick even now to think about what happened. . . .

Suddenly, WHAM! It felt like I was run down by a truck. This guy grabbed my arm, yanked me off the sidewalk, and dragged me behind some dirty bushes in that disgusting park near our house. At first I couldn't see his face as I struggled. Then I recognized him—one of the guards in the neighborhood.

I was so scared. I tried to scream. I tried, Mia! I tried, but nothing came out. Even though it was 90 degrees outside, I felt cold, as if my body—and my voice—was frozen solid. Time stopped as I fought. Then, for some weird reason, I got this incredible courage. I bit the hand that covered my mouth and started to scream . . . louder and louder. He threatened me with his gun and then slammed my head to the ground. That's when I blacked out.

When I woke up I found myself stretched out like a dead body in the grass. My head was pounding, and at first I couldn't remember anything. Then it all came back to me in a rush, and I sobbed. There were scratches and bruises all over my arms and shoulders, and the back of my right hand was bloody.

Then I panicked. He raped me! He raped me! I thought. But my clothes were still in place.

I was so relieved I wasn't raped that I cried harder.

I sat there sobbing for the longest time, my face in the dirt. Then I noticed an old man, maybe 80 years old, kneeling near me. He handed me a clean handkerchief and spoke to me softly. He looked into my eyes and told me things I didn't understand—and yet I did.

He helped me stand. Slowly we walked down the street and back to my house. It seemed we walked for days. Time must have been ticking in a different dimension, because I know it's only minutes from the park to my door. As we came to the outside wall of my house, the old man let go of my arm as I searched for the house keys. I turned around to say something, to thank him, and he was gone. Vanished . . . I looked around. I kept spinning this way and that.

I walked through the front door and the house was quiet. Everyone was in the courtyard playing, and I heard Susanna singing a new song she had learned from Juana. I went into my bathroom, locked the door, and cried. I don't know how long I sat on the floor in a fog, the tears just streaming down my face and onto the tiles. Then I started to feel so gross, so dirty, that I took a shower and tried to wash all the dirt off of me. Tried to wash HIM off of me.

Oh, Mia, I wouldn't hate you. I'm so sorry I said that earlier. I would never hate you. I love you. But you must be mad at me. "Why?" you ask. "Why didn't you run right to your parents? Cry on their shoulders and have them comfort you?"

I couldn't, Mia. I just can't. I'm guilty. It's my fault. You see, only days before, I got another long lecture about how I dress, how I'm so different here, and how I flirt so much. I stand out. I'm a flirt. I admit it. Mom and Dad told me to change who I talk to and how I act. "Women and girls do not wear shorts and T-shirts here!" they said. "Nor do they talk to and smile at everyone on the street!" I didn't follow their advice. I flirted with that guard. All the guards.

God saved me, but I didn't deserve it.

My parents noticed how frazzled I was that evening. They asked how I was. "Tired," I remember saying. I covered up my bruises, wouldn't look them in the eyes. I just crawled into bed.

I remember next to nothing about our trip into the rain forest. I know I complained about everything there, but that's normal for me since I don't like bugs, huts, heat, piranhas, or rubber boots. I was numb and so mad at myself—and anyone who came near me. The whole time I kept thinking about writing you, but I couldn't. For weeks I have been rehearsing over and over what to say, and now the whole story is coming out in a foggy blur.

I wish you were here. I have nightmares. Except they are not nightmares. They come at me all the time, day and night. What if it happens again?

Don't tell anyone! I deserve what I got.

Write when you can. Pray for me.

Gretchen

September 27
Pacific Palisades, California

Dear Gretchen,

I wish I could bring you back here. I'm not even sure where to begin except to say I'm sorry. I'm sorry you're having a horrible time in Ecuador. I'm sorry I can't help. I'm sorry that anything terrible would ever happen to you. Your letter gave me such a shock. It made me want to scream at that guard, to hit him, to run to the police. I can't believe anyone would ever want to hurt you.

After I got mad, I started to cry. I cried as I read your letter over and over. Mostly I cried because you think it's your fault. How can it be your fault?

Gretchen, you are the most beautiful girl I've ever known. Your long golden hair, your tan legs, and confident walk—and a face that could be on any magazine cover. Of course, I know how beautiful you are inside, too, but maybe . . . thinking about it now, sometimes life is more dangerous when you are so beautiful. Maybe you shouldn't smile so much. I don't know. I don't know. . . . I do know that no matter what you wear or how many times you smile, it is wrong for someone to attack you. He attacked you.

You might hate me for saying this, but you've got to tell your parents. You asked me to pray for you, and I have. Each time I close my eyes and ask God to keep you safe and help you feel better, I end up thinking, She has to tell someone, not just me who is a million miles away. I don't know what your parents would say, and they might get really mad, but they should know. This guy needs to be in jail! He could hurt others. Shouldn't the police know so they can get him off the streets? A guard who attacks instead of protects? I just want you to be safe and happy.

I have other news about school and gym, but it doesn't seem right to tell you now.

Please write soon. I promise I won't tell a soul about the attack.

Best friends forever, and please take care of yourself.

Love,
Mia

Fall

October 7
Pacific Palisades, California

Dear Gretchen,

I'm so worried. I haven't heard from you in more than three weeks. Did my last letter make you mad? I didn't mean for it to.

All day today you've been on my mind. I couldn't concentrate at school, and at the gym it was worse. The beam coach finally sent me off to stretch after a half hour of falls. "Mia, you're off in outer space," she yelled. "Go stretch. You'll be safer on the floor."

I left the gym before workout was finished, so here I sit writing you. If I don't, these questions will keep turning in my head, and I won't get anything done. I'm worried that I stepped over the line when I said you should tell your parents about the attack. The very last thing I want to do is hurt our friendship. Please let me know if something is wrong.

It's hard being so far away from you. I feel that even though we live in different hemispheres, no one could ever take your place in my life. Do you know we've never fought? I don't think we've even disagreed on anything big—except maybe what color bathing suit to buy. I still think I look best in black! But no matter, I can't bear to think that maybe I've upset you.

Plus, I know you'll want to hear about Russell. Yes, a boy. So write soon, and tell me we're still friends.

Love,
Mia

October 1
Galápagos Islands, Ecuador

★ ★ ★

Hi, Mimi
Wishes from the sea. It is lovely here,
and I'm thinking of you as I bake my
body brown in the warm summer sun.
I wish you were here so we could
swim together with the turtles.
            Love, love, love,
            Gretchen

10¢
Ecuador

TO: Mia Katawari
1212 Long Avenue
Pacific Palisades, CA
            90272

October 11
Pacific Palisades, California

Dear Gretchen,

I got your postcard today from the Galápagos Islands. I had to look it up on a map, and I wish I could have gone there too! The picture made it look like paradise. But the greatest part about the postcard wasn't the picture. It was your happy words. Should I assume that we are still friends? Yes, I'm going to assume we are still best friends.

So I won't wait to hear from you to tell you about Russell. I don't want to wait, anyway. I met him at school last year, and we bumped into each other a few times over the summer. He is gorgeous. Not that looks are everything! He is on the varsity volleyball team and is very sweet. He is Asian like me, though just half. He is tall and has superbroad shoulders, his eyes are light brown, and his hair and skin are dark. When he talks to me he's a little shy, but not with his friends. And he asked me to go out on a date! Wow! I said yes, and you know, this is my first official date.

This Saturday we're going to have an early picnic at the beach and then see a movie. I'm so excited, yet nervous at the same time. Anyway, here are the big questions, and another good reason for you to write me ASAP! What should I wear? How should I do my hair? What about perfume? I need you here to be my beauty consultant! I'm sure you could give me some good date tips too! Knowing me, I'll be lucky if I take the time to brush my hair and wash the chalk off my hands before he picks me up.

I've left out one small detail. He's not a Christian. I want him to be, but he's not. My parents don't know, but maybe God has brought him into my life for a reason.

I just glanced at the clock, and it's late. My bed is calling, and I need my beauty sleep! I hope you write soon. I'm anxious to hear from you.

Love,
Mia

October 17
Quito, Ecuador

★ ★ ★

Dear Mia,

I should be thrown to the sharks for not writing you sooner. I even upset your workouts—now that's friendship! Thanks for having faith and sending me the news about Russell. That's the best kind of letter to get. One about your best friend and a boy.

I am **NOT** mad at you. The reason I didn't write is because we are all going crazy around here trying to get set in our new schools. We've been all over town—buying supplies, books, lunch boxes, and uniforms. (Can you believe I have to wear a blue, starched uniform? I almost hopped a boat back to the States when they showed me a sample.) My mom has enlisted all of us to help.

Mia, you have helped me so much. Thank goodness you didn't hurt yourself because of my stupidity. I got your letter saying I should tell my parents about the attack before we left for the islands. Did you get the postcard? It truly was the most beautiful place in the world. Just what the doctor ordered—an isolated island, lots of sun, no worries.

Because we were rushing off, I brought the letter with me to read once I could find a place alone. It wasn't until the third day of our trip, when everyone else left the boat to explore an island, that the perfect opportunity came for me to plop myself down and face the truth.

Knowing you as well as I do, I was sure you'd tell me sweetly and simply what you thought about the attack. I opened the envelope carefully, wanting to read your words, but hating myself for the trouble I'd caused. I still felt so guilty for flirting, for fighting with Karen, for not listening to my parents.

My hands shook as I pulled out the familiar yellow stationery. I read the whole letter out loud on the back of the boat. When you said I should tell my parents about what happened, I cringed and almost tossed the envelope and all into the deep blue sea.

After I relaxed my hands and unwrinkled my face, I put your letter down and it all sank in. I started to sob. I must have added two buckets of tears to the seawater that day, because I felt so confused, so ugly, so ashamed, all at the same time. I thought if I told my parents it would make me feel even guiltier for putting myself in that situation. But your words helped me see the other side too, and that even though I was so stupid, that guard still was wrong.

It took me a lot of hours to decide to tell my parents. The last thing I wanted was another lecture. Not another lecture!

The next day when we were out for an evening walk, the perfect opportunity to say something popped up. I hesitated. I turned red in the face. I wanted to curse. I just wasn't ready to talk. But when would I have the chance again? So while Karen, Elsie, and Susanna were off looking for seashells, my parents and I sat and stared at each other.

At first I stuttered and stumbled over the words, but once I got momentum, I gave them the whole story without blinking. They listened without saying a word, even though I could see times when my mom wanted to butt in. But she didn't. Instead she cried.

We sat there for a while after I had finished, and I could see the wheels turning in their heads. . . . It gave me time to prepare for the monster lecture I was about to get.

Now here's the incredible part. The first thing my mom did was pray. She said to God, "Thank you for keeping Gretchen safe and unharmed." My dad hugged me and asked if I was okay. He held me for a long time and it felt sooooo good. I wouldn't have called him crazy then for anything. Then we talked about telling the police when we returned. I said I would if they thought it would help. That was it, no lectures, no lectures!

From that moment on my parents have looked at me differently. Like I grew up in one day. I can't explain it, but I changed in their eyes, not in a bad way, but still changed.

Before I say any more . . . HOW WAS YOUR DATE? A picnic on the beach sounds so romantic! I'm sure you looked perfect—your long, black, shiny hair glowing as it always does, and your exotic eyes and creamy skin. You don't need me as a beauty consultant. Someday you'll realize how incredibly beautiful you really are. Everyone knows it except you!

What did Russell wear? What did you talk about? Did you enjoy the sunset arm in arm? Did he kiss you good night? You better write me soon, and tell me all the details. I'm starved for some good, clean romance.

In a way I suppose I had my own romance on vacation, but instead, mine was with sea turtles, dolphins, and blue-footed boobies! The trip to the islands was a dream. We were there for eight days, and all we did was eat, swim, lie in the sun, and see incredible things. Everyone was so happy, and there was no fighting, no biting, no bickering. How can you argue about snorkeling or watching sea lions? The crew of the boat was hilarious and treated us like royalty.

Now back to reality. School has started for me too. So much for the sound of the waves. I'm going to a private high school, where everything is taught in Spanish. It has been only a week, and there's not much to tell (except that my uniform is less than flattering), because I am totally confused about everything as soon as I step through the school door. Most of the other foreign kids in the city go to the International, the British, or the American school. We're too poor, my parents said, for those schools. Besides, they want us kids "immersed in the culture."

Who knows how it will all work out? I'm not sure I want to hang out with all those rich, foreign kids anyway. We've met a few of those families already, and the kids my age are unbearable. Always talking about skiing in New Zealand and how their servants practically dress them. Nobody like you, Mia, nobody. Church is a little different though. I'll tell you more about that later.

One last thing before I put the pen down and slobber all over the envelope. I have never seen that guard since the attack. He's gone, and I think he's gone for sure. We did go to the police, and they took down all of the information (it took forever!), but they can't find him. That old man probably made him vanish too.

With that, it's time to say good night. You're the best friend in the world.

Much love,
Gretchen

October 28
Pacific Palisades, California

Dear Gretchen,

I am so happy you are doing better. I'm especially glad that you told your parents about the attack and that they didn't lecture you. And I'm sorry that I worried about our friendship. I won't do that again.

So, THE DATE. You want to know, right? I know you want to know! I'll tell all. . . .

I actually spent some time getting ready and twisted my hair into a long ponytail. I put on lip gloss and just a touch of blush on my cheeks but decided to forget the mascara because I always smudge it and my lashes are already black. I wore a new, soft yellow sundress that I got at the little boutique on Seventh Street. With it I wore flat leather sandals. It made me think that adding a few dresses to my mainly leotards-and-sweats wardrobe would be a good thing.

I was worried about my left hand though. On the Thursday before our date I had a lot of bar work at the gym, and my hand ripped. It was a bad rip too, tearing off half the skin on my palm. I kept imagining Russell and I walking down the beach at sunset and him getting grossed out when he tried to hold my torn hand. On Thursday and Friday nights before bed I smeared my hand with this tea-tree-and-jojoba-oil concoction that I found at the health-food store. Then I wrapped my hand in a sock while I slept. God certainly works miracles, because this is the first time I've had a rip heal in only two days!

Russell picked me up at my house and said hi to my parents. Johnny was also at home, hovering around the corner, pretending to be a devoted big brother but really just there to tease me. Russell was shy but polite when my mom asked where we were going and when we would be home. I pushed to get us out the door before Johnny started grilling the poor guy like he threatened he would. It's incredible that we made it out to the car without too many embarrassing moments.

Russell drives a light blue VW Bug, his first car,

and he's so proud of it. He bought it only a couple of months ago, and he washes it almost every other day. It's horribly noisy but fun, and it's so old you can see the street through the floorboards. He said when it rains, water comes up through the car if you drive through too big of a puddle. The car's name is Suzie.

So Russell, Suzie, and I headed for the beach with a picnic basket in the backseat. His mother must have packed the basket. At the beach he opened it and pulled out all sorts of Chinese favorites: dumplings, rice, and shrimp. We ate with old, wooden chopsticks and drank green tea from plastic cups. We dug our feet into the sand and talked about our lives as athletes. He sees volleyball as a way to break into a world he has never known. His family has had some problems, I guess, and he wants to make something of himself. I'm sure he will.

We took a walk along the shore, splashing one another. We looked for sea lions and blue-footed boobies, but no luck! I wanted to do cartwheels, of course, but couldn't with the dress on. It's almost impossible not to tumble with all of that empty space in front of me. Then we headed for the car so we could make it to the movie on time. On the way to the car he caught my hand in his. Everything was so beautiful, him included, and I can still remember every moment and every word we said.

The movie was crummy, but because I was with him it didn't matter. He loved it—some James Bond adventure. When the credits hit the screen, I jumped up so fast to leave the theater I must have startled people three rows back. Russell took the cue, and we raced out the back door and into the night.

We didn't have much time before I needed to be home, so we headed straight for Suzie. She buzzed us back to my house, and we sat in the car for a minute before going up to the door. "Can I kiss you?" Russell asked me, and for the first time in my life, I kissed a boy without being dared to do it! I've filled my life with gymnastics and school, and this kiss felt like I was finally experiencing real life.

My cheeks felt flushed, and his lips were so warm. I can't believe I'm telling you all of this!

I know you're enjoying it though, because you were always trying to set me up with someone from church to make my life more romantic. How many times did you say, "He's cute, and you'd make a great couple, Mia!"

After our one kiss he hurried me to the front door, where we said good night. I told him that I had a wonderful time, and he said the same. From the way he stared into my eyes, he looked like he really meant it and wanted to stay longer but knew that it was time to go.

Good thing he left when he did because Johnny threw open the front door just as Russell was driving away. He started teasing me like only an older brother can, but I held my ground and didn't tell him a thing about our evening!

Well, that's it! My first date, kiss and all.

That was last night, and today is Sunday. I just got home from church with my family, and this afternoon Russell and I have plans to meet down at the beach club to play paddle tennis. I'm nervous just thinking about seeing him again. It's one thing to kiss someone in the dark after a romantic evening, but it's another thing to see him after and think the feelings are still the same.

. . . I'm back. It's late, and I really should be in bed, but I want to get this finished so I can mail it in the morning. I don't want to disappoint our mailman, Woody. He's been our mailman since I was a baby and is practically a member of our family. We always give him Christmas and birthday presents, and he will sit on the front porch and drink a cup of coffee with my mom if he's not in a big hurry. You've probably seen him before. Anyway, he delivers the mail at about the same time that I get home from school and always asks, "Something going to A-Q-DOOR today, Miss Mia?"

Boy, do I get offtrack sometimes!

Russell and I played two sets of paddle tennis at the club. Then we sat on the courts and talked and talked. We talked about last night and how much fun we had on our picnic. He wanted to know more about my family and seemed amazed that we were all happy and liked each other.

At some point, we made our way to the beach

and walked out on the jetty. Leave it to me to stumble on the rocks and practically crack my head open. He saved me, sort of, but I still made an amazing fool of myself. We laughed, and I said that's the trade-off for me. Elegant on a spring floor at the gym and hopelessly clumsy everywhere else! Oh, well, better for him to know sooner than later!

That's enough of Russell and me. I want to hear more about your school. And I'm proud of how you told your parents about the attack.

Thanks for telling me I'm beautiful. I needed that. And I miss you.

Love,
Mia

P.S. Next week is my first meet. I feel ready, but pray anyway that I'll give a solid performance. It'll be in San Diego and a good time to check out the local competition.

November 3
Quito, Ecuador

★ ★ ★

Dear Mia,

What a romantic date! I loved the part when Russell asked if he could kiss you. I read it over and over again. That color yellow must have looked so gorgeous on your dark skin too. Oh, good grief! I missed it all!

You should see the kids I'm meeting at school. What were my parents thinking sending me there? I'm sure torture wasn't high on their list, but every day I go through torture—pure torture. After the first week, things have gone from mildly okay, to sort of bad, to horribly horrible.

First of all, I don't speak Spanish, so I feel incredibly stupid. I stare at the teachers, who could be talking Russian for all I know, and they stare back at me, not knowing what in the world to do with this blank-faced American. Every night I go to sleep and pray that somehow God will give me the gift of . . . Spanish! It is almost funny how ridiculous the whole situation is. Or I should say it would be funny if it weren't my life! My parents are asking me to be patient. They say I'll pick up the language soon. I'm worried that I'll be 20 years old and still in eleventh grade.

Today was the same as every other day. I spent the morning trying to break the language code as the teachers walked around the classroom, lecturing and checking on everybody's work. My brain began to freeze up after about an hour of unsuccessful thinking. Then I started to daydream and get sleepy, and the teachers gave me dirty looks, rolling their eyes and throwing up their hands. They are much more dramatic down here than in the States.

What goes on in the classroom is bad, but what happens outside of the classroom is even worse. Then I went to lunch. Supposedly I am an alien or smell or something, because no one wants to be near me. I have learned to sit in the corner and watch all of the girls talk about me right in front of my face. They know I can't understand. It's so obvious they don't like me, and I know they want it to be obvious. They even point at me, each one turning her head around to look at me and laugh.

The boys are not as mean. They just look at me and smile, but because we can't communicate, a smile is all the company I get. One boy, Jaime, tried out his English on me, but he struggled so much with the words, he gave up after just a few phrases.

It has been two weeks at school, and I'm already wondering how I'm going to get through an entire year.

As a family we're doing well. I haven't fought with my sisters for weeks, and Karen, Elsie, and Susanna all like their school. They are going to the local school near our home, but they go together, so they have built-in friends. One of the teachers is a sweet lady, Señora Manzana, who spent five years in Texas as a child. Her English is very good, even though she says some words like y'all with a Spanish accent. Weird! She is spending extra time at lunch tutoring them. It makes me want to be in grade school again, so I could be with them.

Apart from school, I've gone the last two weeks to the church high school group on Tuesday nights. Shannon Johnson comes, even though she's already 18. I already feel welcome there and have made a few friends.

There are two girls that I like especially, Tina and Marguerite. They came to speak with me right away, and instead of talking about themselves, they asked me all sorts of questions about how I came to Ecuador and where I'm going to school. They told me about a retreat the high school group is having next month and said they would like it if I would come. How sweet of them to invite me personally. I still haven't asked my parents. I'm waiting for just the right moment.

Another highlight of the youth group is Matthew Montrane. I haven't said much to him except hi and bye. I can see that some of the girls already have a crush on him, and it's no wonder. He is something . . . no, he's much more than something.

He's 16, I found out, like you and me, but I thought he was 19-going-on-20. He has sandy blond hair, which waves in soft curls, and he always sweeps one curl with his right hand. His green eyes are so bright, so green, they catch you off guard, so you can't help staring straight into them. His jaw is broad, and his lips are red and full. Wow, I haven't studied him, have I? His clothes are incredible. He wears silk shirts and shoes that must come from Europe.

But it's his smile that melts me. His whole face lights up when he smiles, and wherever he looks it's like his eyes have laser beams that cut right into your heart. At least that's what happens when he smiles at me! He knows he has all the girls wrapped around his little finger, and he reminds me a bit of Steve because he's always goofing off but never getting in trouble. I couldn't keep my eyes off him. (I sure hope I can control myself better next time I see him.)

Tell me more about Russell when you get the time. Have you been on many more dates? Are the two of you "going out"?

I better go. I'm baby-sitting tonight because my parents have a meeting at the Johnsons' house. I have to make sure all the girls eat Juana's dinner. Susanna always passes her food off on everyone else, and she's such a skinny little runt, she needs me to pester her.

Keep on flippin'!

Love,
Gretchen

November 13
Pacific Palisades, California

Dear Gretchen,

Hi! I was sad to hear of your horrible time at school but happy to hear of your new friends at church. Maybe thinking about Matthew will help you forget about those immature girls. I sure feel for you, but I feel sorry for those girls too, because they have to live with themselves.

I also have good news and bad news, but I'm not sure where to begin. I'll start with Steve.

Steve was out surfing early one morning last week. From what I've heard, the water was crowded because of the large waves. He stayed in as long as he could, but finally needed to head for shore to make it to his first class on time. As he rode in on the last wave, another surfer cut in front of him too close. The other guy fell, and his board flew out of the water and struck Steve in the forehead. The impact of the board knocked Steve out, and he started to drift down into the water.

Two surfers dove to his rescue, and thank God, Steve had his leash strapped to his foot. They hoisted him up on his board and brought him onto the beach. Thankfully, there was a lifeguard on patrol who started CPR and called for help. He was able to get the water out of Steve's lungs and start him breathing before the ambulance showed up. Steve came to on the beach, but he was confused and didn't want to talk.

I went to see him at his house the day after the accident, and he still seemed strange. I can't explain it. He's fine, can speak normally, and remembers everything, but he is so quiet and subdued that I'm not sure what to think.

At one point when we were talking about school, tears welled up in his eyes. I didn't know what to do. I wasn't sure if I should pretend I didn't notice, if he would be embarrassed or what. But I was so touched. I've never seen Steve—our friend Steve— act that way before. So I just said everything was going to be fine and grabbed his hand and gave it a squeeze. I think he appreciated it. Then I tried to move the conversation on to silly things, making him laugh about the day I got saved by the lifeguard.

Steve's up and around now, but he hasn't been back to school yet. I'm going to go visit him again tomorrow, so I'll let you know how he's doing. I'll make sure and tell him that you say hello.

On to better news. Much better news. I WON! I took first place in the All-Around at our first meet of the year. I had a super competition and surprised myself with an awesome score. I won beam, which is almost a miracle. I took second on vault, won bars, and took third on floor exercise. It was strange. I was so calm during both days of competition.

I should thank my mom because she has helped me so much this year. This summer she and I had some great conversations about my life—beyond gymnastics. I've been nervous during competition in the past, so she thought if I focus on the big picture and try to extend my faith into the sport, maybe I could become a more complete athlete.

Now I've been spending some time in prayer each morning before competition, and I really think the quiet time has helped. Plus, just having the attitude that I've done my work and now the competition is in God's hands relieves lots of pressure from me. I do my best, and I know whatever the results, I gave it my all.

This win qualifies me for Regionals in Hawaii. The next two competitions are not very important so it's only a matter of staying healthy until December. The competition there will be tough, but if I perform the way I did at this first meet, I should place well.

Things are going great with Russell!

I sure do miss you. Best friends forever.

Love,
Mia

November 21
Near Otavalo, Ecuador

★ ★ ★

Dear Mia,

I'm writing from my bunk bed. It's early, early Saturday morning, and all the other girls are sleeping quietly like babies. We have a big day ahead of us, and if today is anything like yesterday, I'll be writing for days!

We drove here (the church retreat, remember?) yesterday after school, and I really am not sure what part of Ecuador we landed in, except I know we headed north toward the market town of Otavalo. At some point we left the highway and bumped up and down on a dirt road for what seemed like a month. They don't really have YMCA camps here, so we are staying at a private hacienda that someone in the church owns. It's kind of like a lodge the way they have it set up.

The reason I'm up so early is because I never got to sleep. . . .

I'm sure I told you about Matthew Montrane in my last letter. He is the gorgeous one. And . . . he is the first boy to keep me guessing at every turn. One second I am falling in love with him, and the next I am furious and shaking my fists at him.

Matthew likes me. He made a point to sit by me on the bus, bullying his way past Marguerite and Tina, announcing my great fortune at being near him. We talked during the entire bus ride, and he told me about himself and his family. I'll tell you more about them later. We sat in the very back, and every now and then Tina or Marguerite would turn around and give me a "are you okay?" smile. I was fine.

When we arrived at the hacienda, he helped me off the bus and carried my bags to my room like a true gentleman. He asked if I would sit by him at dinner. I said yes, and so we were together every minute from the moment we left Quito.

We had time to pass after our last meeting of the night and before the counselors expected us in our rooms. It's obvious Matthew knows this hacienda well, because he took me walking through unmarked paths and away from the lights of the house. He grabbed my hand and started to run with me. I was laughing all the way and begging him to slow down before I fell—I'm not much for skinned knees or muddy clothes. But then we arrived at an open area near a stream. I started to sit on a small bench, but he caught my hand and asked me to dance! I laughed.

We danced a waltz while he hummed what he said was the music from Swan Lake. I remember that because he said, "You're as beautiful as a white swan on a glassy lake." I wasn't as graceful as a swan, but at least my dad had taught me to waltz. After spinning us around our outdoor ballroom, he tightened his grip around my waist, dipped me back, and asked, "May I kiss you, mademoiselle?" I told him I was not in the position to say yes or no with my head dangling so close to the ground. He lifted me up, as if I weighed nothing, and kissed me anyway. Mia, can you believe there are boys in this world who are so romantic? It must be something Latin.

I was ready to get back to safety, and yet I could have stayed there dancing with him all night. Surprising as it is, the more practical side of me won out. I said thank you for the dance, but it was getting late and I didn't want to be in trouble my first night out. We ran back to the cabin and I scurried inside like a mouse.

I whispered to Tina as we were getting into bed that Matthew is crazy. I asked her if he was always so full of nonsense, and she nodded a big yes. "Just don't let him bowl you over," she said. And with that, I tried to go to sleep, but of course, I've been tossing and turning all night.

It's funny. I didn't even think of the attack—of being alone with Matthew with no one to save me—until I started trying to sleep here in my bunk. I think it's because I feel so safe in his arms, as if he cares about me like a mother would care for a child. It felt good not to be afraid. But I am afraid that here it is morning, and I probably have enormous black bags under my eyes!

Who knows what this day will bring, but if Matthew continues to sweep me off my feet, I'm bound to have lots more news for you in the next letter. I'll send this one off today and write again as soon as I get home.

Romance is in the air,
Gretchen

November 23
Quito, Ecuador

★ ★ ★

Dear Mia,

It's Monday afternoon and I just got in from school. I read your letter and am horrified to hear about Steve's accident. Please tell him I'm thinking about him.

You are so awesome to win your first meet of the year! I can't imagine what it feels like to be a gymnast. I can hardly do a cartwheel without killing myself. Flying through the air, spinning and twisting, and still landing on two feet! You're amazing!

I have good and bad news for you too. . . .

You've probably already received the letter I sent you from the retreat after my sleepless night. Matthew continued to "bowl me over" all weekend just like Tina had warned. I didn't heed the warning though. The good news is I enjoy his craziness. I like being overwhelmed. He's funny, gorgeous, charming, and full of surprises.

He must have told his family about me the minute he got home, because—here comes the bad news—our entire family is going to their house for Sunday brunch this weekend! His mother called mine today, and they set it up while I was at school. First, I'm mad at my mom for not asking me about it, and second, I'm scared to death to go to his home and meet his parents. Will his parents like me? Will he still like me?

I haven't told you much about his family yet, but they are beyond rich. They have a house in the city, where Matthew's father spends time doing business. They have an old hacienda in Cumbaya, which is about 20 minutes from our neighborhood of Quicentro, and that's where his mother stays most of the time. They also have a house on the beach, and who knows where else they might have one, not to mention the cars, boats, and airplane.

We are invited to visit them at the hacienda, and from what I can guess, it's an incredible place. They have so many servants Matthew couldn't even count them all. His father is an oil bigwig, who grew up in the States. His mother is Ecuadorian, but her family came from France way, way back—and I don't know what she does.

Help! How am I going to get through this week without cracking up? What will I wear? What will I say? The more I think about it, the more nervous I get, so I'll just have to tell you about it once it's over. At least this will give me something to think about while I'm wasting away my days at school.

Thanksgiving is coming soon, and we've been invited to the Johnsons' house for dinner. It will be strange to be at school that Thursday. I'm looking forward to the Thanksgiving food, especially having one meal without rice. Mashed potatoes sound like heaven to me.

My mom gave both Juana and Stella Thursday, Friday, and Saturday off. She told them they have been working so hard that it would be nice for them to spend some extra time with their families. You should have seen their faces when she told them. Señora Juana argued, saying she didn't need extra time. Stella smiled and said it would be nice to go home to help her family. They live near a town called Ibarra, and she said it takes her hours to get there on the bus.

Well, I hope you have a nice holiday with your family. Hug Steve for me if you see him, and give your little brother a smooch on the cheek. (I know how Charlie loves my kisses!) How's Russell? I'll write again soon and tell you how the brunch goes. I'm getting butterflies just thinking about it.

Love,
Gretchen

December 5
Pacific Palisades, California

Dear Gretchen,

Hi! I'm sorry it has been so long since I've written. After a full day of school, four hours at the gym, homework, and sometimes dinner, I wonder why anyone would ever fight going to bed. I brush my teeth, splash some water on my face, and that's about all I can manage before I collapse onto my pillow.

All of the hard work is certainly paying off, though. My grades are good, and I have done well in all of my meets this season. I told you I won the first meet. Then I took second at the second meet, and last weekend I won the third. Confusing, huh? Oh, and things are patched up with Jamie. We talked a while back, and she apologized for calling me stuck-up. I pray I'm not. . . .

In 10 days I'm off to Hawaii. There will be seven gymnasts from our gym, plus two coaches, traveling together. I'm looking forward to the time away.

School will have finished for winter break, so we're staying in Hawaii a little longer to tour around and play on the beach.

I'm still dating Russell, and I guess you could say we're "together." We don't see each other as often as I would like. I finally have a boyfriend and I never get to see him! He's busy with volleyball, and you already know how full my life is. I've been trying to get him to come to church with me, but that hasn't worked yet. On the Sundays when I don't have a competition, we meet down at the beach club in the afternoon and play paddle tennis. But no more rock hopping. I can't afford a cracked-open head right now.

Last time we were down there I set up my camera in the sand and we took pictures together. I'll send you some. We also saw Steve at the club last Sunday, making sand castles near the water with his little sister, Robin. They had a whole city in progress. They had made little houses, each with its own swimming pool and cocktail umbrella. The sand streets were lined with Popsicle sticks as sidewalks and trees made of seaweed bulbs.

Russell and I sat down and helped for a little while, and Steve and Russell talked about volleyball. Russell wants Steve to come back to the team. I think Steve would rather build sand castles right now than play volleyball. I didn't hug Steve as you asked, but I did tell him that you said hi.

It's so weird. Steve's just not the same anymore. I've seen him quite a few times since the accident, and he's definitely not as spunky as he used to be. The doctors say he's fine. That he suffered a very minor concussion and now can go back and do all of the things he likes to do. But I'm not sure he has totally healed. At least not emotionally.

He's not dating anyone right now. I don't know what happened with Adriana, but they broke up a long time ago, even before the accident. He is spending a lot of time with his family. I guess I miss the old Steve, always clowning around, always getting into trouble, always making fun. I don't quite know what to do with the new one.

I better go. I have an English paper to write. I read David Copperfield by Dickens. Have you read it? It's excellent! Anyway, reading it was one thing, but writing about it won't be as easy. Wouldn't it be great if I could just hand in one of these letters and get graded? Maybe not!

Don't forget to tell me all about your trip to the hacienda for brunch! Is love still in the air?

Best Friends,
Mia

December 12
Quito, Ecuador

★ ★ ★

Dear Mia,

Love is swirling wildly around in this South American air. What a brunch we had at the Montranes'.

You know me. I spent two hours getting dressed, changing clothes over and over, until I had the perfect outfit on. And the day before I buffed my nails, scrubbed my feet, polished my shoes, plucked my eyebrows, and ironed my dress. I'm so crazy about the way I look that it even makes me laugh sometimes.

I was the last one to hop in the car, and I talked nonstop the first 10 minutes of the drive. Finally my dad said, "Gretchen, please . . ." I knew what he meant, so I kept my mouth shut for the rest of the trip.

A guard stopped us at the gate. Once my father explained who we were the gates swung open wide as if by magic. We drove down a long, long road to a gravel drive near the front of the house. Matthew's house. I practically started to shake when I saw its size.

A man was waiting for us, and he helped us out of the car, then drove it away. Another man came and ushered us to the front door, where I stood looking at the mansion in amazement. The front door alone was amazing. It reminded me, almost exactly, of my bed. It was made of the same dark, tropical wood, and it had exotic birds carved around the edges. As I was staring at a corner of the door, where there was a carving of a macaw, it swung open. Matthew and his mom came rushing down the stairs to greet us.

Mrs. Montrane is just as beautiful as Matthew. She is tall and graceful, and is the one who gave Matthew those bright green eyes. It's obvious that she doesn't have an ounce of Indian blood in her, and that's typical, Marguerite said, of the wealthy in lots of Latin American countries. She moves like a queen, waving her slender hands here and there, making her bracelets jingle with every movement.

They met us with shouts and hugs and kisses before they led us into the house. They were so loud you could hear their voices ring through the house, across the stone floors, up to the ceilings, and in and out of every window. I was proud of my normally quiet parents, who rose to the occasion and were as spunky as I have ever seen them. Karen, Elsie, and Susanna were sweet and behaved themselves. The biggest thing was keeping them from giggling too much. Once they get started, their giggles are impossible to stop.

Matthew grabbed my hand right away, led me through the entry, and into the parlor, where his father was waiting for us. The room was packed with books and papers and furniture of all sizes. Mr. Montrane—a big, cowboy-looking man with graying hair and a soft, whispery voice—was sitting in a leather chair near a wall of windows that looked out at their stables and a pasture. There were horses grazing not too far away, and Matthew explained that they had polo ponies and a polo field. Can you imagine?

Mr. Montrane stood up to greet us, and then came the surprise of the day. A little girl, only seven years old, ran past the window, waving. She disappeared from view and soon you could hear her footsteps echoing through the house until she burst through the doors, looking embarrassed. She jumped into Mr. Montrane's arms. He gave her a quick kiss, then scolded her about being late. I didn't even know Matthew had a sister!

Isabella was dressed in jeans, riding boots, and an old T-shirt. She must have been out playing with the horses. Matthew's mother gave her a kiss too, then sent her to change. She was so cute and shy. So different from Matthew.

We walked to the courtyard where the grown-ups sat down. When Isabella came down, her mother introduced us. Isabella had washed her face and changed her clothes. She immediately hopped into Matthew's lap, where he kissed her, tickled her, and even rearranged the clips in her hair. He was so sweet with her. At one point he had both Susanna and Isabella bouncing and laughing, each on a knee.

We had brunch in the courtyard at a table that stretched for miles. There were flowers everywhere, even some in little vases near each plate. Forget the paper napkins and plastic forks—everything was silver and china and breakable! I kept waiting for Elsie or Susanna to drop a crystal glass on the stone patio, but thank goodness, it never happened. The food was wonderful too. My favorite thing was a crepe filled with sweet cheese and strange South American berries. I could have eaten a million of them, but I held back and ate two.

I sat next to Mrs. Montrane, who asked me questions about school and how I liked life in Ecuador. She made a comment about my long, blonde hair, saying, "How refreshing it is to see something other than brown or black." She has red hair, almost the same color as little Isabella's flowing curls. She told me, "Once we realized Bella would be a redhead, I ran to the salon with the perfect excuse to have red hair myself."

It does look beautiful on Mrs. Montrane, but Isabella's hair is the most gorgeous shade of red I have ever seen. The color is so deep, it almost looks like the red could rub off on your fingers if you were to touch it. I would love to sit down and brush it and braid flowers into it, but I get the feeling she probably cares more about her horses' hair than her own.

When we finished eating, Matthew's dad suggested the grown-ups take a walk in the garden, while the kids run and play. Isabella and the girls headed for the stables, and Matthew asked me if I would like to see some more of the house. Before I had time to answer, he had me by the hand, dragging me from room to room. For whatever reason he is always running me everywhere.

It was easy to get lost in such a big place, and I got turned around, thinking east was west, after about two rooms. I remember a gym, a movie theater, and an enormous kitchen. The ballroom was my favorite. I wanted to stay and dance another waltz with him, but instead,

Matthew whisked me off upstairs. On the second floor were the bedrooms and guest rooms, and that's when we ended up in his room.

Matthew's room is enormous, with views to the garden on one side and to the polo fields on the other. It was neat and organized, and there were fresh-cut, tropical flowers on a side table. It wasn't like any boy's room I have ever seen—no basketball hoops over the bed, posters of football players, or clothes thrown all over the floor. When I said something about it to him, he just laughed and shrugged. He obviously had other things on his mind, because the next minute he was kissing me.

It takes a lot for me to feel uncomfortable, but shivers started to run down my spine. Being there alone in his room—an adult sort of room—and feeling so charmed by him, I was more than uneasy. So I pushed Matthew away. I said it would be more polite to ask for a kiss first instead of always stealing them. He told me I was the most beautiful creature he had ever seen in Ecuador. Those words almost did me in. After all, it had been a long time—and never in Ecuador— that someone had given me a real compliment.

I remember looking into his gorgeous green eyes and feeling dizzy and dumb. I couldn't have said anything smart or witty or even halfway intelligent when I was standing there in his arms. He tried kissing me again, and wow, was I thankful when I heard the sounds of the girls running through the halls downstairs and calling our names. From the look on Matthew's face, I could see he was thinking the same thing I was—so we hurried down the back stairs.

When we found the girls, Matthew pretended like we had come from the kitchen. I was relieved to be with my sisters again. Before long we were back with my parents and our visit was over.

I like Matthew so much. But I have never known a boy who is so confident, so handsome, and so . . . I don't know the word. He "bowls me over." Tina was right. I'm not sure if I mind or not. It's nice to be with someone who is so sure of himself. On the other hand, I feel so unsure of myself when we're together. What I really want is to talk to him. Find out how I fit into his life. All I can think about right now is how much I want him to fit into my life!

Christmas break is coming soon for me too. I sure wish I could meet you in Hawaii for a dip in the Pacific. I need to work on my tan! I won't have much of a break, however, because my parents have hired a Spanish tutor. She will be spending three long hours every morning with me. What a way to spend a holiday.

Do you think Matthew could be my Romeo?

Love,
Gretchen

December 19
Oahu, Hawaii

My dearest Gretchen,

It looks like I'll have a lot more time on my hands to write. . . .

Before I totally blow you away with my news, I want to tell you how much I enjoyed reading your last letter about your trip to Matthew's house. I have it here with me, and I keep reading it over and over again. To know that my best friend is so happy saves me from thinking more about my pitiful state.

Merry Christmas to you and your family. I hope you all have a wonderful holiday together. I hope all of your dreams come true. I hope Matthew will be your Romeo because I'll need as much good news from you as you can share. Happy news, anything, just something to make me smile, to make me forget.

It is beautiful here in Hawaii. We finished the competition on Sunday and I placed second, barely behind Sarah Bensing from Oregon. She's also rated as one of the top 10 gymnasts in the nation. I almost beat her, but I didn't land my dismount on bars as solidly as I should have. That little bit cost me first place. But to be truthful, I was thrilled with my performance and didn't mind coming in second.

The part that I do mind, however, is that I am sitting in an armchair, my foot propped up on four pillows, with 10 pounds of ice wrapped around my right ankle. I have been here for at least four hours, and as I watch my ankle swell, I know that this is it. I am finished.

I have already cried enough to last a lifetime. At least enough to last for four hours. I know all the symptoms of this injury, and I can see Dr. Grant shaking his head at me when I walk through his door next week. I already know the answer. This is the end—no more gymnastics.

We were walking along the beach and I twisted my ankle. That's it. That's how I did it! Walking! Oh, Gretchen, at least I could have gone out in style. My ankle just rolled over and I heard the fatal rip in the ligaments. It didn't hurt much, because as the doctor says, "The nerves have already done all their cryin'." I know it's a bad tear, though, by the amount of swelling that's happening before my eyes.

Tonight I'll call my parents. They already know how well I did in the meet. I can't stand the thought of calling them so soon after the competition and breaking this ugly story to them. One of my coaches keeps telling me, "It's not that bad. You'll be back in the gym and ready to train for Nationals next week." But she's always saying crazy things, and I hardly believe her for a moment. My other coach hasn't said anything. He just drifts in, shakes his head, and walks out. I don't need them or their advice anymore. I know I'm done.

Help me look at the bright side. Now I can go skiing . . . I can stay out as late as my parents say and not as late as my coaches say . . . I can eat anything I want . . . I won't have to worry about which scholarship to pick . . . I won't have to miss school to go to Nationals . . . I won't be able to try out for the Olympic team. . . . Oh, this is not helping me see the bright side. I must not be done crying yet.

I hate to depress you, so I'm going to say good-bye. Please pray for me. Pray that God can find a new life for me, would you? Pray that I don't go throw myself in the ocean. Pray hard for me, because I feel the tears coming again. Pray hard. Pray really, really hard.

I love you and I miss you, Gretchen. I do.

Mia

Winter

December 27
Quito, Ecuador

★ ★ ★

Dear Mia,

I just got your letter from Hawaii. When I saw the postmark from Oahu I squealed, knowing you had won your meet. I rushed into the courtyard where everyone was eating, and I read the news out loud . . . well, I read the first line but then stopped.

"What, Gretchen? What is it?" everyone asked. "Did she fall? Didn't she make it to Nationals?"

"She made it," I said. "But she's not going." I lost my temper a bit. LIFE IS SO UNFAIR! I beat the ground over and over again, then finally finished my tantrum and told them about your injury.

Here I am now at my desk, wondering what to write, my fists aching. I can hear bits of conversation floating up from the courtyard, through the open balcony door, and into my room. They're saying the same things I'm thinking. "Maybe the doctor will say it's nothing. Maybe it's a different injury that will heal in no time." We've got to be right. I want you to be in the Olympics so badly! I want to say, "Look, there's my best friend, Mia, beating the leotards off those skinny Romanian girls!" I'm so sorry for you.

I'm afraid to ask about your Christmas. Ours was quiet. We set up a tree in the living room and decorated it with ribbons, lights, and wooden birds. I spent Christmas Day with my family, but I got to spend the evening of the 23rd with Matthew.

Somehow it doesn't seem fair to talk about Matthew though, when you're so down, but you asked for happy news in your letter. He's happy news all right.

Matthew's on my mind round the clock. School is more bearable now that I can occupy my thoughts during those long hours of incomprehensible lessons. For now, I don't see him except on Sundays. We're at different schools and he hates the phone. He's an old-fashioned Romeo. "When I speak with you, I want to see into your eyes and watch your beautiful lips move. On the telephone, I can't see your lovely face." Pretty goopy stuff—on paper.

We've gone out every Sunday afternoon since The Brunch. Last Saturday I had planned to watch him play polo, but then came the dreaded last-minute phone call. Something about the driver. I sat on the couch for hours, all dressed up, still clutching my purse, visualizing how hand-some he must look riding about on his majestic horse. Pooh.

When we do go out, he first calls my parents to ask their permission, and then they ask me if I want to go. "Are you crazy!" I tell them. I don't know why they bother asking me. Certainly they can read me after all these years. And of course, my parents think Matthew is a dream for being so thoughtful.

Then he picks me up (he has his own car and driver) and we drive, shop, and stop at cafés. He seems to know people everywhere he goes, but I haven't met any of his school friends yet. Last Sunday we sat and talked for hours. It was heaven.

I've learned he has two passions: music and polo. He rides daily and studies piano and classical guitar. He'll hum or sing anything for me, anywhere. His voice is mellow and clear, and when he sings in Spanish I swoon!

I can only stand so much polo talk before I change the subject. Until I actually see a game I'm going to forbid any more of this-team-versus-that-team talk. He says he wants to teach me to horseback ride because he "loves the way women look on horseback with their hair flowing in the wind." He is always saying sappy things like that. "Stop," he will say. "Don't move. Look how beautiful you are with that light shining over your shoulder." Except when he says those things to me, they don't sound sappy.

Once when we were out, I tried to get him to talk about us. He laughed as he always does and said it's silly to talk about such things and better to simply experience them. But I wasn't satisfied. "Can I say you're my boyfriend?"

He laughed again and rubbed his hand against my cheek. He said, "Of course you can!" Strange. I really didn't know what he would say, despite the kisses.

Well, I think that's enough of Matthew for now. He took me to a Christmas concert, but I'll save that for another letter. I find it's hard to write about him when I know you are there, sad, and I'm here unable to do anything to cheer you up. I want to give you a hug so desperately!

I'll also tell you about Señora Leon, my Spanish tutor. There's nothing like spending your Christmas vacation doing grammar drills.

And by the way, how is your Romeo?

> Sent with much love for my
> very best friend,
> Gretchen

January 3
Pacific Palisades, California

Dear Gretchen,

Thanks for the letter. You're a good friend. But
. . . my life is a mess. You are gone. Gymnastics is
gone. Russell is gone. Just a few weeks ago everything was perfect.

Dr. Grant looked at me and started to cry! This
is a 200-pound football player turned orthopedic
surgeon. His hands are bigger than I am, and here we
are in his office and he's crying. He has been a part
of my life for so long, he's like one of the family.
Once he got ahold of himself, he said, "Can't fix it
this time. You've gotta stop or you'll end up a crip-
ple. You're only 16." He looked at me with eyes
that were begging me to understand. I won't argue
with him.

The injury is not that bad. Well, that's not
exactly true. The injury is bad, but the pain is
nonexistent. I've been casted so many times (this

will be my seventh, but who's counting?) I can do handstands on my crutches. It's never going back into that gym that is making me crazy. I have four more hours a day to kill and feel lost with the extra time.

And there are so many big questions. What are my goals now? Where will I go to college? Who am I without gymnastics? My dad keeps telling me, "Slow down. Take each day as it comes. God has big plans for you, but you've got to let go of the old ones in order to see the new." Easy for him to say.

Russell is another matter. It's amazing how all the bad comes in big, ugly lumps. I don't know if this will make you laugh, throw you into shock, or seem totally normal.

He wanted to sleep with me.

We were on the phone, and he asked me if I would go to bed with him! He thought we were getting to know each other well enough and that it was time to move our relationship forward. That's forward all right. All I could do was break down and cry!

Thank goodness I had the cordless. This was not a conversation I'd want my parents to overhear! I went outside and tried to explain to him that sleeping with someone is not in my plans for a long time. In fact, I sort of have that slotted for my wedding night. He laughed at me and said that was ridiculous. It hurt me when he laughed.

We must have talked for two hours, but the conversation never went anywhere. I tried to convince him that waiting is worth it. I told him I had decided when I was 10 that I wanted to try to always choose Christ's path for me, even if it was a hard road. An uphill road, even, or a road where everyone turned left, but I had to walk to the right. I wanted Russell to know what being a Christian means to me. That sin is real, that blessings are also real, and that there are reasons—good reasons—for the way I do things. He was shocked and mad. It was like talking to a brick wall. Now I know why I never should have gotten involved with him in the first place.

That was it. The last thing I told him was that I am sorry. Somehow I must have misled him. How could he think I would ever do anything but kiss him? I feel so ashamed.

My family has been sweet to me. They know that Russell and I have broken up now, and they are spinning around like dust devils trying to pull me out of this gloom. I'm trying hard too, but I only succeed for a few minutes, and then I'm back sinking deeper into depression. But I don't want you to be gloomy as well, so I'll tell you about my Christmas.

As you already know, every year on Christmas Day our family drives to my cousin's house in Malibu for a big party. They live on Point Dume. I'm sure I've never taken you there, because we only go the one time each year. Their house is just steps from the beach. We talk and eat and then go for a walk along the shore right before sunset.

This year was the same, except I can't walk! So my dad hoisted me onto his back, his strong arms holding my one good leg and one bad, and off we all went down to the water. He must have carried me like that for an hour. I'm not light. I'm little, but I'm not light. The sunset was awesome. I had my family all around me and everything felt okay. I looked out at the water. It helped to feel small yet secure, standing there on the shore. That was my Christmas.

I love hearing about Matthew, but I have a hard time imagining that a boy like him exists. He sure is spoiling you! Would you send me a picture of you two? Which reminds me . . . I have those photos of Russell and me, but I'm only going to send you one. I'll get Charlie the Tuna to take some more of just me. He's pretty good with the camera. Speaking of my little brother, he's not so little anymore. He has grown almost five inches since you left for Ecuador. I know Karen had a crush on him. You can tell her that he is more handsome than ever.

Time to go. It was Charlie's 15th birthday yesterday, but we're celebrating it tonight. I still need to wrap the present I have for him. It's a stuffed toy cockroach. His room is so messy I thought it would fit in perfectly with his "decor"!

Love,
Mia

Dear Mia,

Russell didn't deserve you—that's obvious! And you're going to get some big bonus points for sticking up for what you believe. It may not seem like it now, but someday he'll understand your point of view and kick himself for letting you go.

Here in Ecuador everyone thinks Americans are just like the people in the movies. Always having affairs, living in mansions, doing drugs, killing each other, and driving fancy cars. Maybe that's what Americans really are like, except for you and me. Maybe most kids do have sex when they are 16. But that still doesn't mean we need to! What if you got pregnant? or got AIDS? Did Russell ever think of that? Send me his address and I'll set him straight!

I can tell you're struggling, Mia. I want to be there with you so I can help fill up those extra hours every day. I'd keep you so busy your head would spin. But there must be a reason I'm not. Believe in God's timing. Easy for me to say,

I know. But I'm just telling you the same thing you told me when I was feeling down.

Well, I might as well fill you in on the sunken-boat story. It seems to be an ongoing soap opera. My parents traveled to Guayaquil last week to speak with Capitán Garcia. After the ship was hauled from the harbor to a boatyard, my parents and el capitán opened some of our crates. They weren't waterproof . . . . all of the books, files, and papers are ruined. That was harder on my parents than I think they had imagined. Some of my mom's best paintings have been transformed into soggy sea art. And it will take a fortune to rebuild my dad's book collection.

A few things of mine survived. A crystal cup that my grandma had given me is still in perfect shape, and some of my jewelry looks like it got a real good cleaning. Elsie's favorite doll survived, but boy does it smell! My Toscana shoes are somewhere in the dump.

The end of the story will come when the insurance gets sorted out, but thankfully, I hardly know what insurance means.

I know enough about insurance that I'd like to have a policy on Matthew. I want insurance that he will call every day, visit me every other day, and never go away for more than a week. I still haven't told you about the Christmas concert, have I?

A few days before Christmas a package with my name on it was delivered to our house. Inside was a note and a dress. The note said "Pick you up at seven for dinner on the 23rd. You are a jewel. Love, Matthew."

Mia, I wish I could show this dress to you. It's silk— a dark, emerald green silk—and the cut is perfect. It has a round neckline, is sleeveless, and the hem comes to just above my knees. I've never felt so elegant and grown-up in my life. I showed my mom the dress and, wow, did she look worried! It took time, but I finally convinced her with talk of how it's a Latin thing to give gifts for this or that, and please, not to send it back—that they would be offended if we did.

Then she made a complete turnaround. We realized I needed hose and shoes to match. She took me shopping the same day, even though she was in the middle of a painting.

Matthew and his driver picked me up as the sun was setting, and we drove to Chez Maurice, where his parents and Isabella were waiting for us. On the way there he gave me yet another surprise. We were sitting in the backseat, holding hands, when he pulled a box out of his jacket and said with that paralyzing smile of his, "Open it, sweet Gretchen."

I tugged on the paper, and the top of the box fell into my lap. Inside was a string of pearls. He gently put them around my neck, kissed me, and said, "Perfect. Now you look perfect. Merry Christmas."

When we pulled up at the restaurant I was still in shock. I stumbled up the curb, and his mother met us at the door with a hug and kiss. She whispered in my ear, "My, what a handsome couple you two make!" Matthew winked at me. It felt good to be a part of their family.

After dinner we went to a private drawing room for the Christmas concert. The room and the people in it sparkled with gold and jewels. Our seats were up front, within feet of the musicians. But it didn't matter where you sat. Once the music started, the notes filled every space in that room. The music swished around, and the sound was so overwhelming and so full it felt as if it would soak right into my skin. I can't explain it, but I have never felt that way about anything before. It was as if my blood and bones, toes and fingertips were all listening. Between Matthew and the music, I was swept away to another world that until then hadn't existed for me.

Parts of my Christmas break were amazing because of Matthew, but in reality, most of my break was spent side by side with my Spanish tutor. Señora Leon is from the school and could easily be mistaken for a drill sergeant. She arrives at our house at exactly 9 A.M., on time. She heads straight for the kitchen table, sits down, and pulls out a miniature clock, which she sets directly in front of me.

First, we talk in Spanish about whatever. Life, food, sisters, Ecuador—it doesn't matter. That lasts for half an hour. In the beginning she corrected every other word I said, and it drove me crazy! Then comes a half hour of grammar. At 10:30 exactly we take a 10-minute break, and Juana brings Señora Leon some Nescafé and I get lemonade. The same every day.

The last hour and a half we do drills. She asks me questions, and I ask her questions. What boredom! But it's helping. So who am I to complain? Didn't I ask God for the gift of Spanish?

Now that school has started again, Sergeant Leon—I mean, Señora Leon—is tutoring me three times a week.

I better go. This letter is so long. I'll keep my fingers crossed for good news from you. I agree with your dad. I think God has big plans for you. Just hang in there, Mia. Just hang in there.

Love,
Gretchen

January 19
Pacific Palisades, California

★ ★ ★

Dear Gretchen,

Hi. Thanks for the words of encouragement. I'm trying to get out and do new things, and I actually went to a high school basketball game on Friday night. I think it's the first school event I've ever had time for.

It was stupid. Here I was with all these kids I've known since kindergarten, but I have no idea who they are. . . . I guess they don't really know me either. Russell was there and that made it worse. I left just as everyone was making plans to do whatever you do after a basketball game. I was glad to go home.

My friend Carol and I have been spending more time together. She and Stuart are still dating and still sailing the Hobie Cat. She is very involved in the church youth group and even helps with the younger kids when she can. She picked me up the other day, and we drove up the coast to the beach club. They make the best chocolate-chip shakes, so we each got one and sat on the beach (me with my foot hoisted up to keep the sand out of my cast) and listened to the waves. I wish you could have been with us.

Tomorrow I'm supposed to stop by the gym and clean out my locker. I told the coaches I would be there, but I think I'll ask my mom to do it. She hates driving all that way to the gym, but I think she'll make one last trip if I ask her. I really don't want to cry anymore, and I know I will if I see everyone working out as if nothing has changed. Well, nothing has changed for them.

I've got homework to do. Biology. Tell me more about Matthew. I like your stories. What songs were played at the concert? Maybe some music like that could help me forget my misery. You must have looked like a princess that night. Write soon.

Love,
Mia

P.S. Did you show your parents the pearls?

January 26
Quito, Ecuador

★ ★ ★

Dear Mia,

I'm baby-sitting again, and Elsie and Susanna are in bed. Karen is doing her homework. I've already finished mine, but I'm in the mood to write. Sometimes when I write you, it clears my head.

You know, after reading your letter again I can see how you're trying to keep your head up. I'm proud of you. I think because deep down you are such an optimist and always the first one to spread sunshine to others, incredible doors are going to open up for you, even without gymnastics in your life. I know I'm far away and can't do much to help, but my heart is there with you. If you ever need a shoulder to cry on or a hand to hold, mine can reach all the way across the world if you need it.

Matthew's loving hand, however, seems to come and go with the changing tides. I struck up the nerve this morning and called him. I was anxious to see him, so I reminded him of his promise to take me riding. He sent the driver right over. As we pulled into the drive, there Matthew stood—and he wasn't smiling.

I could tell right away that something was wrong. But when I asked if everything was all right, he changed his mood, smiled, and turned into his old cheery self. It was like that all morning. One minute he was laughing and having fun with me. The next minute he looked depressed, like his thoughts were on the moon. I'm worried because I have never, ever seen him like this.

After he led me around on the oldest horse they own, he told me to go wait for him in the courtyard. I went and sat under an umbrella and waited. I waited and waited . . . I must have been there for an hour when I finally heard footsteps and turned around to see Mr. Montrane coming my way. He asked for Matthew and furrowed his brow when I said I didn't know where he was. I waited some more, but the only one who showed up was the cook with a pitcher of lemonade.

Mr. Montrane joined me after a short while. He spoke to me of his life. He said his real love is music—not oil, not money—and that he grew up in a small town in New Mexico, lived in a small house, and never had big dreams. His whole life in Ecuador happened by accident. He also said that he liked having me around and thought I was a good friend for Matthew. He hoped I was happy spending time with him, and I said of course I was.

When Matthew didn't show up after another half hour, Mr. Montrane went to find him. I heard them talking in the house. I couldn't hear exactly what they were saying, but I knew from the tone that Mr. Montrane was less than pleased.

Matthew came out alone and apologized for having left me for so long. When I asked again if everything was all right, he said nothing was wrong, but that it was time for me to go. I didn't want to leave. I wanted to spend the whole day with him. But he insisted, so he called the driver.

As I climbed into the car, Mr. Montrane came running out of the front door with something in his hand. He leaned in through the car window and handed me two Bach CDs. He had sort of a sad smile on his face and said, "I saw how much the music affected you the night of the concert. Sometimes when I'm confused, I can find much peace in music. You're a dear girl, and I'm sorry Matthew was not the gentleman he should have been today."

I'm playing the music now. . . .

I feel like calling Matthew and asking him what's wrong. I said nothing to make him upset with me.

I keep forgetting to tell you that Stella, our maid, has invited Karen and me to her home. There is a local holiday next month, so she has four days off. I've been begging my parents to let us go with her, but they aren't sure about having us be so far from our home here. But Stella and I have become fast friends since my Spanish has improved. She is so quiet and so simple, almost majestic. I'm just dying to go and find out what her home and family are like. I know her prince is there, and I want to find him!

I'm tired. Karen went to bed a while ago, and I should too. We have to be at church bright and early. I'm wondering whether Matthew will be there. Bye for now.

Love,
Gretchen

P.S. My parents don't know about the pearls, and I've decided not to tell them. I'm not sure they would understand. I hid them under a stack of your letters stuffed in the back of my armoire.

February 7
Pacific Palisades, California

Dear Gretchen,

Everyone is trying to help me—more like feeling sorry for me—and I can't stand it anymore. My mom thinks I should learn to knit. My dad says I would be a good golfer and has a program ready for me as soon as I get my cast off. The neighbors are suddenly calling me to baby-sit, and my old tennis coach, from when I was eight, thinks I should try out for the high school team. I guess she hasn't noticed that the bottom half of my left leg is wrapped in fiberglass! If they would all just leave me alone . . . I've never had so much attention in my life. They must think I'm about to crack up or something.

Well, maybe I am. I haven't felt happy about much of anything in weeks. School is weird now that I have nothing else to fill my day with, and seeing Russell is torture. I'm sure he has told everyone in school why we broke up. I know I did the right thing by ending the relationship, but I didn't think it would be so hard.

You know, the toughest part about my life is that I wrote the whole book years ago and this is not the ending I had in mind. The ending chapter was not titled "Girl Ruins Gymnastics Career on Beautiful Hawaiian Island." My ending was "Girl Marches into Olympic Arena Ready for Hot Day of Competition." I didn't even want to win. That was not in the book. I just wanted to be there, wearing the U.S.A. warm-up, ready to give it my best.

What in the world will the new ending be?

Gretchen, I never thought I could be so depressing. I reread these words and feel like I'm dumping a bucket of mud on you. I'm sorry. Maybe I should start to knit or golf or try out for the tennis team in my cast. At least it's coming off soon. Next letter I promise I will be happier. I miss you.

Love,
Mia

February 13
Quito, Ecuador

★ ★ ★

Dear Mia,

Just now as I was reading your letter, I got a thought. I have never known you as Mia the gymnast. I have only known you as Mia. I have never seen you compete, except for that one time on TV. I don't even know where your gym is/was.

It's not that I don't care about those things—it's just that there's a lot more to you than sports. You are my best friend, and I still need you whether you are a gymnast or not. So don't crack up on me like you said you might. . . . Who would read all of my crazy letters? Who would listen to me without laughing? I love you, Mia. I just want you to know that.

And today is no time for laughing. Matthew hasn't called in days. He hasn't been at church or at youth group. I called twice to see if I could talk to him, but both times the secretary said that he was out playing POLO! He has never called back.

I called Tina to ask if he has been at school, but she was no help. She said he has been there every day and that I should forget him. I'm getting desperate. I love being with him and, well, I thought he liked being with me. Why else would he buy me a dress, pearls, dance with me, kiss me, take me out . . . treat me like a Juliet?

If he hasn't called by tomorrow, I'm going over there. I'll ride the bus all the way out to the hacienda and make him talk to me. I'll go nuts if I don't.

I'll write again tomorrow and let you know what happens. . . .

Until then,
Gretchen

February 14
Quito, Ecuador

★ ★ ★

Dear Mia,

I am such a fool. I am such a fool. I am the fool of all fools.

I told you yesterday that I was going crazy not hearing from Matthew. I haven't seen him since the day we went riding, and NOW I KNOW WHY.

I went to his house today after school. It took a million buses just to get there, and then I walked for a mile or more before reaching the gate. I should have taken a taxi, but I was out of my mind and didn't even think of it until now. When I arrived at the house, all hot and sweaty from the journey, the guard recognized me and let me in. He must have called up to the house because there was Matthew, waiting by the front door, watching me walk the long way up the gravel drive. He stood there, laughing.

I told him we needed to talk and his smile faded. Instead of heading through the front door, we went around the side of the house to the pasture and into the stables. We found a bench outside one of the horses' stalls, and I sat down, still breathing hard. "Why haven't you returned any of my calls?" I asked. "Why haven't you been at church? Don't you care about me? Aren't I a part of your life?" I was babbling like a two-year-old, and he just let me go on and on. "What about the dress? and the concert? and the pearls? What does it all mean? I'm so confused!"

At last I asked him what I really wanted to know. "Where do I stand with you?" I surprised myself by being so blunt, but I suppose it had been building up for a while. All along, ever since I met him, I never really knew who he was or why he did things. He always seemed like a big, beautiful puzzle just waiting for me to put together. Well, I got all of the ugly pieces put in place today.

His lame response was, "I'm so sorry. I didn't want to hurt you. I saw you were new, new to everything. New to Ecuador, new to the world, and so beautiful. I wanted to make you feel like you belonged here. Didn't you like the gifts?"

"The gifts? So you were just doing me a favor? You always give pearls to newcomers?" I cried. "And what about that day. I want to know. That day when I sat in the courtyard for hours waiting for you!"

"I was talking to my girlfriend on the telephone."

"Your what?" I looked at him with tears streaming down my face. "Your girlfriend?" I must have repeated "your girlfriend" 10 times before he said anything.

I dropped my head in my hands and let the tears roll. He started to run his fingers through my hair, and I jumped up and yelled, "Stop. What are you doing? Stop touching me like you own me!" He was surprised and then went into this big, long speech about how he likes me but only as a friend. He thought I knew that. He has a girlfriend and they've been going out for a year. Didn't he mention her? She goes to his school.

Right now I can think of a thousand names I should have called him, but when he told me, I just sat there staring at him like a dunce. "A girlfriend? You already have a girlfriend?"

I stood up to leave, but he caught my arm and pulled me back down onto the bench. He wanted to make things right. He started to talk about how everything was a misunderstanding, that I don't know yet how things really work in Ecuador. He sure got that part right.

I stood up again and walked away. This time he let me go. As I reached the stable door, I blurted out, "What about the kisses? Is that how friends kiss in Ecuador?"

And in typical Matthew fashion, he just smiled and said, "You are so beautiful. How can I help myself?"

UGH!

I walked past the stables, past the front door, down the long gravel walk, and out the gate. It was getting dark, but I was furious. I got to the bus stop and waited. It wasn't long before Matthew's driver pulled up in front of me and told me he'd take me home. I said no way.

But then I felt funny about being out on the street alone. It must have been because my emotions were running haywire, but suddenly the day of the attack came flooding back into my mind and over my body, as if it were happening all over again. I felt sick. I slowly opened the door the driver had offered me. I cried all the way home.

So here I am, sitting at my desk feeling like a fool. I am a fool. Why couldn't I see he was using me? It's amazing how I can see it all now, how it all fits together. I was his little project. When he wanted a girl on his arm, I was a phone call away. But not my phone call, HIS. What a lame Romeo.

So that's it. How can I face anyone at church again? They watched it all happen, and they let it happen. I bet they knew all the time how it would end up. Ugh, this place. Just when I'm starting to like life here, everything gets ugly again.

What should I do with the pearls? Throw them to the swine? What a happy Valentine's Day! Write soon.

Love,
Gretchen

February 23
Pacific Palisades, California

Dear Gretchen,

It's horrible. Your letter is just horrible. You must be feeling so awful, so angry, and so hurt about Matthew. I'm so sad for you. Why is it that when I'm up, you're down, and when you're down, I'm up? I can't wait for the day when we're both happy and carefree. That's how I feel today, believe it or not. Happy.

My family has been so loving, so supportive, and such a living example of how much God loves me that I can't be depressed anymore. And what a blessing it is to have dinner together as a family again, to laugh at the table and not worry about rushing off to workouts or racing to get my homework done. But enough about me.

You know, I really liked reading about your adventures with Matthew. But now he's the one really losing out, not you. Gretchen, you are such a wonderful girl—I can't believe he wouldn't give up the world for you. (Why do those words sound so familiar?) But maybe Matthew is so spoiled he won't ever understand real life and real feelings, or perhaps he just needs time to grow up.

Thank you for the CDs. I play them in my room, with the door closed, and try to imagine the glittering drawing room and the music swirling around me. It's a new experience for me to hear music that isn't the length of a floor routine. I like it. You were so generous to send them all the way from Ecuador when I could have just run to the music store here.

You asked about the pearls, and I think you should decide what to do with them. He gave them to you for Christmas, right? Now, if you will never wear them because they make you think of bad times, then maybe you could sell them and give the money to someone who needs it. Or just give them back and say it was too generous a gift . . . I don't know. Do what your heart tells you is right.

Write soon. Let me know how you are doing, and if you've talked anymore with Matthew. I miss you.

Love, Mia

March 2
Quito, Ecuador

★ ★ ★

Dear Mia,

Your letter made me think of Matthew. How he has
hurt me, how he has spoiled my life here, how he strung me
along like a wooden puppet. But it isn't the end of my world.
I'm too stubborn for that. Blessings can pour from unex-
pected places, I've learned, and they don't always have to be
wrapped in silk or studded with pearls.

Let me tell you about my trip to Stella's house. It was a
miracle that my parents let Karen and me go, but I know
they trust her, probably more than they trust me! We had
an amazing time. What a change from hanging out at
Matthew's hacienda.

The bus ride to Ibarra was cheap (not even a dollar)
and smooth. In Ibarra we changed buses and headed for
somewhere near Stella's village. This bus I have to tell you
about. . . . It was ancient, and the driver played loud Latin
music the entire half hour we were on it. He had rosary
beads hanging from his giant rearview mirror, along with

tassels, banners, pictures, and figurines. His name, Miguel Angel de Napo, was carved into a wooden plaque, which hung over his head.

He drove like a maniac, like most people in Ecuador, but it was as if he were driving a Porsche instead of a 50-year-old "Chevy" bus. More than once I reached for a nonexistent seat belt so I didn't have to brace myself from falling into Karen or Stella. All three of us were smashed into one seat like sardines.

The highlight of the bus ride was THE LANDSLIDE. The driver said something in a language that was not Spanish. Stella translated and told us to "hang on!" Instead of having us get out and taking the bus over the landslide empty, he must have thought it would be fun to four-wheel it with 50 screaming passengers. The truth is, Karen and I were the only ones screaming—for everyone else I'm sure it was just another bus ride in Ecuador.

We headed straight up the landslide, the engine roaring at all the boulders we had to bounce over. Then Miguel made a sharp turn and raced back down the mountain with the brakes screeching and the tires slipping all over the place. There was a hole in the floorboard of the bus right by my feet, so dirt spit up onto my shoes and all over my legs. I can't believe we made it to the village alive! You read all the time about these buses plummeting over cliffs or down ravines. It's not hard for me to imagine that happening anymore.

The village was quiet, clean, and peaceful. We were the only ones who got off at Stella's village, but I shouldn't even call it a village because it was just four whitewashed houses clumped together in the middle of nowhere. On the road to her house we passed fields where they grow potatoes, bananas, and all sorts of other things.

Five minutes later we were standing at the front door to her house. This house was a bit bigger than the other three. Basically it was a little, white, wooden hut on stilts. I think they build the houses high to keep out animals or maybe water or maybe both, but I never asked.

We were immediately greeted by Stella's little sister and a funny dog who came bouncing down the front steps of the house. Her sister, Mina, looks just like Stella. Mina is sweet and Elsie's age. We went inside the house, where I met Stella's mother and another woman who lives with them.

We all spoke Spanish, but from their halting speech, it was obvious they didn't normally speak Spanish at home. I asked Stella what language they usually spoke. She said they still speak the old Incan language, Quechua.

We cleaned the grime off our faces with water from an old battered metal bowl, and then Stella took us on a tour of their land. Karen and I couldn't believe the pure beauty of it. In every direction there were so many colors and shades of green, and there were plants and trees trying to grow everywhere. The view of Cotacachi (an enormous volcano) was incredible too, much prettier than Pichincha, the volcano visible from Quito. There was no smog to block the view or high-rise apartments to get in the way.

And there were birds everywhere! They live in the banana plants in the forest that borders their land. Stella told me some of the names, but the list was endless. Hummingbirds, jays, tanagers, woodpeckers, but most of the birds I have never seen or heard of before. Their land is noisy because of the birds, but it was a noise that I liked. Much better than beeping horns and whistling guards.

We didn't eat rice once. That was great. But we ate potatoes with every meal. A good change for a few days. The people here grow their own food and don't eat much meat. They eat fruits and roots and vegetables. They make a barley mush mixed with brown cake sugar, which sounds horrible, but is delicious. They also cook with leaves and herbs from the forest. Not once did they run to the market for something they needed. Not that there was a market! Can you imagine living without a grocery store nearby?

In fact, there is nothing nearby. They knit their own sweaters from llama wool. They make their own sandals from old rubber tires. They build their own furniture from trees in the forest. They even get their water from a well that they dug. They don't have much, but that is so silly to say because they have everything they need and more.

Of the four huts on their property, one is for cooking and storing foods, two are for sleeping, and the fourth is for other relatives or whoever extra might be living with them. At night we slept in a hut with Stella and Mina—Karen and I in one bed, Stella and her sister in another.

The beds are raised, wood platforms. Stella showed us how you pile wool blankets and llama hides on top of the platform to make it soft and warm. Then you lie down and pile another 10 or so blankets on top of you. Since it was freezing up there at night, sleeping together was a good idea. Sleeping was the easy part because we were cozy. It was getting up in that cold morning air that almost killed me.

The first evening, right before dinner, Stella's father and brother came home from the fields. We were setting the table on the porch of the cooking house. They both carried machetes and were dressed alike: a dark blue poncho over a white baggy shirt, white pants that came just below their knees, rubber sandals, and a wide-brimmed felt hat. Stellio, Stella's father, and Modesto, her brother, both have long black hair pulled into a single braid. Just like Stella, her family is beautiful.

We were all introduced. I especially liked meeting Stella's father. He shook my hand and wished me well. I noticed that he said every word carefully, like he was giving a toast at a party or making a speech in front of a crowd. Karen shook his hand too, and when she looked at Modesto, she melted. Yep, she fell in love right there on Stella's porch. I looked at her and watched it happen. Her face flushed and her eyes started to blink funny, like she wanted to look at him more but shouldn't. From that point on Karen watched his every move and hoped he would look at her or speak to her.

It's not like our trip was a vacation because we were always busy helping with some chore or another. We did get to see a lot of their property (they have over 50 acres of land given to them a long time ago by the Catholic church), and we spent time in the forest gathering plants, nuts, and other things for meals.

One afternoon we took a break from chores, and Modesto drove us to a spot where there were ruins. He had found them by accident when he was doing a lone pilgrimage to Cotacachi, that volcano which is always looming over you wherever you are. "I went to the summit to ask God for direction," he said. "How long did it take you?" I asked. I thought he would say, oh, a day or two. "Three weeks," he said. He said he was deciding between university in Quito or staying on the farm. I didn't know if it would be right to ask him about his experience, but God must have told him to stay on the farm.

The ruins were incredible. It was difficult to see much at first because of all the plants. But as Modesto started hacking away with his machete, he showed us the foundations of what he thinks were temples built with stones so big it would take a thousand men to lift one. How anyone could have moved these things is beyond me. And they are all put together like pieces in a jigsaw puzzle, with hardly a line between each stone. He asked us not to tell anyone about the place, for fear that someone would want to take advantage of it. But I sure would love to show you!

He also took us to an old irrigation canal that the Incas had built to water their fields. You can barely make out its shape except at the start of it, where Modesto says he spends one day every week rebuilding it. It would help them a lot on their farm to have a constant supply of water, and he thinks it will take him at least 12 to 15 years to finish. Imagine starting a project knowing it will take you a quarter of your life to do it.

Karen's crush on Modesto grew and grew the more he spent time with us. She followed him around like a little puppy dog all weekend. He was always kind and patient with her blabbering, but poor Karen is wasting her time on him.

I found this trip to be liberating in so many ways. One— I was so busy I never thought about Matthew. Two—I didn't put a drop of makeup on my face or worry whether my hair was clean or brushed or dirty. Three—I didn't look in a mirror for four days. Now there's a record!

I looked everywhere for Stella's prince, but I'm sorry to say, I couldn't find him. We did find Modesto, though, and he is definitely a prince, just not Stella's. If I weren't so mad at Matthew, maybe I would fall in love with Modesto too. He really does belong in a fairy tale.

Maybe it was the music—or maybe it's his humble, godly way of being—but one night he played a flute for us when we were sitting on the porch after dinner. I closed my eyes to listen, and when I opened them, I looked in his face and saw a real prince. Bands of gold circled his wrists and neck, his clothes were colorfully woven, and he held an intricately carved staff in his hand. The image fit him beautifully.

The last thing I want to tell you about our trip is how God opened my eyes about myself. I realized two things so strongly that it almost made me sick to think that's how I've been acting my whole life!

I am so into the way I look on the outside that I have no idea what sort of beauty I have on the inside. I'm always worrying about how my hair looks, whether my clothes show off my figure or if my lips are the right color. What a waste! I've never asked myself what sort of friend or sister or daughter I am. Or if I'm making any difference in this world to make other people happier.

The other thing I realized is how selfish I am. I don't go out of my way for other people. I do things for myself. I care about my time, my clothes, and my feelings. But what about Karen? Shouldn't I share more with her? Or Elsie? Shouldn't I spend more time with her? Stella makes little knitted dolls for Mina just to make her happy. Modesto repairs a thousand-year-old irrigation canal, not just for him or his farm, but for the children he might have someday and for the villagers all around him.

How in the world did it take me so long to see these things in myself? I don't want to live in some fancy hacienda and have servants wait on me and spend three hours in the bathroom every morning getting ready. Ugh! I feel like this trip helped me make some real breakthroughs in my life. Things I think God's been waiting for me to see all along—only I've been blind to them.

Thank goodness we didn't have to take that crazy bus back to Quito. Modesto drove us into town because of a meeting he already had scheduled. Karen was flapping her eyelashes at him the whole trip. He was very sweet to her and answered all of her questions even when she was asking silly things like, "How many acres of banana plants do you have?" I tried hard not to laugh. She just wanted to keep him talking.

But the closer we got to Quito, the quieter Stella became. Now I know why she is shy at our house—Quito is not her world.

I've run out of energy for now, so I'll say good-bye.

Much love,
Gretchen

Spring

March 13
Pacific Palisades, California

Dear Gretchen,

I'm so happy to hear there are places in the world where you don't need a grocery store to survive! Your trip to Stella's home sounds like a dream, but I don't think anyone in California could live there for more than a week. People from the Palisades would probably starve right in the middle of 50 acres of potatoes because they couldn't figure out how to dig them up!

Guess what? I made the tennis team. I haven't played since I was eight, but I think the coach had pity on me and gave me some extra leeway. When my cast came off at the beginning of February, Dr. Grant said, "Take up swimming, will you?" I'm a horrible swimmer so I thought of tennis. I wear air casts each time I put on my tennis shoes, and both ankles feel stable. I lost my first two matches, but I'm having more fun than I thought was possible at school.

And . . . other things are happening to make my life a little brighter.

I bumped into Steve in the halls at school one day, and we stopped to talk for a minute. The bell rang for class to begin, and he made me wait while he pulled something out of his backpack. It was a white envelope with a red ribbon tied around it. We both ran off to our next class. I had English that period with Mr. Gunderson, and there was no way I could have opened the letter during class. If Mr. Gunderson found it he would have made me read it aloud like a Shakespearean play in front of everyone! So I waited, and during my last class of the day, biology, I opened it while the teacher was giving out the next day's assignment. The first line starts:

> Dear Mia,
>   If you're in class, close this letter and wait until you are sitting under a tree or rubbing your feet in the sand. I don't want my words to be confused with a teacher talking about frog eggs or something else.

I closed the letter and went directly to the beach after school.

I'm going to just copy the whole letter for you

because it speaks for itself. I am in such shock. I can't wait until you've read every line. Here goes.

I know everyone thinks that I have changed since my surfing accident. I suppose I have. But some friends have suggested that it's a physical change, like something in my brain went pop! And now I'm a different person. It's tough to explain to most people, and to be honest, I haven't really tried because I know I'll be misunderstood. Except by you. I think you will understand me and maybe more than that, I think you might be able to really see into me, once I make a few things clear.

I bet you thought this would be a love letter, by the way I wrapped it. Well, it is. But you'll have to wait for that.

When the surfboard hit me, my life changed. I woke up on that beach, with people hovering over me, hoping I was alive. I knew the minute my eyes opened that I was a different person, like I needed a tragedy, an excuse to change. This was my chance. I know it doesn't make much sense, but I liked games. I liked playing games so much I played them with God. I wanted to see how far away I could get from him, how many stupid things I could do, without ever going over the edge. Living on the edge, that's what I was doing. It was a spot between total rebellion and halfhearted obedience.

For a long time I have been questioning myself and the choices I would make, the places I would go, the friends I would hang out with. Sometimes I felt like I had trapped myself into a world that I really didn't like. Partying, saying the "right things" to be cool, dating all the girls, and yet I had this longing to change, to ask God for forgiveness, and to grow up. So that's where I'm at now. I'm trying to grow up.

Which brings me to you.

First of all, I heard all about your injuries and what that means to your career in gymnastics. I am sorry that a door has been closed on an avenue in life that I know you enjoyed. But because of where I'm at, I'm not so sure that closed doors are such a bad thing. It's good to feel the hand of God moving, and I know God wants to move in your life. You've proved that in who you are. I've been watching you these past few months, and I can tell you are struggling. But even in the midst of your pain, I see your efforts to be positive and move forward. I admire you.

You came to visit me after the accident when no one else did. You grabbed my hand and tried to console me when I was at my worst. I looked in your eyes that day and realized I had never really noticed your sweet face or heard the purity in your voice. I saw a godly young woman. I decided I wanted to watch you, to pray about you, and to pray for you.

I'm giving this to you because I want you to know that I love you. I love you like a friend and a sister. But I would like more. My heart tells me I want more. I want to know you and to love you better. I want to spend time with you, go on walks with you, talk to you.

What do you think? Do you think I'm crazy like everyone else does? Are my words pure nonsense? Or does this all fit together for you like it does for me?

I'll be at the beach club this afternoon. I'm guessing that's where you'll be. I'd like to speak to you after you finish reading this letter. But I don't want to scare you or embarrass you. Look for me down by the jetty if you feel like talking. Otherwise I'll just be patient and wait to hear from you whenever you feel up to it. I'm hopeful that you'll find me.

Your brother and friend,
Steve

Can you believe that letter? Isn't it so beautiful? It explains so many things about Steve and the way he's been acting these last few months.

I walked down to the jetty and there he was, sitting on the rocks! We hugged, my fingers still gripping the letter. I was embarrassed when I looked into his eyes, knowing his feelings for me. But it felt so good to be there, and I was really happy for the first time in a long while. Happy because he has changed and happy because I felt like I was about to. Like when I'd chosen to walk out of Russell's life because he'd wanted me to do something that wasn't in God's plan for me, that God had noticed. And that he'd had a wonderful surprise all ready for me, if I could see my way clear to find it.

Steve and I must have talked for two hours out there. We talked about big things—not school, not gymnastics, but how life is changing for us and where we fit into the world. It felt so good to have someone think my life was getting better because a "door closed." It's like Steve has let his soul come to the surface for me to see. And I loved what I saw. Most of all, I saw somebody who loved God . . . and loved me. Somebody who wanted to follow what God had in mind instead of what he had in mind. Somebody who understood all the questions I'd been going through for the past few months, because he'd been asking God the same ones.

It got chilly out on the jetty and he gave me his sweatshirt. We could have stayed there all night except both of us needed to get home for dinner. As we were leaving, Steve said, "Mia, I'm so glad you came. I really want to know you better. How do you feel? Is this all too much for you?"

It felt strange to be so honest with someone. But I jumped right in and told him I was a little over-whelmed at the moment but that yes, of course, I would love to spend time with him. He kissed me on the cheek and I went home.

What do you think? You know Steve. We have all grown up together. I wish you could talk to him now.

Okay, I'm saving the biggest news for the end. My mom has invited you to come and stay with us this summer. It's already March and summer will be here before we know it. What do you think? You could bring pictures of Stella's house and tell me all the little things you must have left out from such an incredible trip. We could go to the beach and cook dinner for our friends and laugh together about silly things. I miss you, and I loved the last letter you wrote. God is blessing us right now as we try to grow up.

WRITE SOON!

Love,
Mia

March 19
Quito, Ecuador

★ ★ ★

Dear Mia,

Hola, mi amiga! I just read your letter about Steve. I can't describe my happiness for you and him. It was so beautiful it had me in tears! He sounds like a different person, yet I could hear his heart talking. I'm so happy for you, Mia.

I'm packed! Or could be in no time! But is your mom serious? Is it true that she would want me there for three whole months? Your house is so quiet. You bring me into it and—watch out! You better double-check before I wine and dine my parents.

What fun just thinking that the summer might actually come. I would run three marathons back-to-back just to have school over tomorrow. Here's why.

After the trip to the mountains with Stella, I returned to school Monday morning. The bell rang, and I cringed as I sat down in the only open chair near a group of girls who have been less than nice to me in the past. It was obvious they weren't listening to the teacher. As I sat there, I suddenly realized that I could understand every word they spoke! Their words—all their slang and expressions, everything—registered in my brain. I stared at them as they talked about me. They laughed at my long, blonde hair and said I must have been raised by a prostitute. Then they said how stupid I looked just staring at them with a blank face. "She was raised by a monkey," one of them sneered.

Mia, can you imagine? I understood everything they said. For so long I have been living in this deaf and mute world, and finally something clicked and Spanish became like English for me.

The girls didn't expect this. I know I didn't expect it of myself. I stood up and grabbed the hand of the girl who had just called me a monkey. Everyone in the room noticed and turned to look at us. At this point I didn't care anymore about the extra attention. I was so angry, so sick of feeling out of place, that I pulled her to her feet, waited until she looked me in the eyes, and then said slowly in SPANISH, "_Amiga._"

I waited a second to make sure she was listening before continuing in Spanish. "Friend. Do you really see me as a monkey? No. I'm a girl just like you. Not perfect. Just a

155

girl. I'm tired of feeling alone at this school. Tired of being mistreated."

I waited another moment to gather my thoughts. "Jesus teaches us to see beauty inside ourselves and in others." Then I started to cry. "We can love or we can hate—it's our choice. Let's you and I choose what's right. Let's . . . be . . . friends."

I said the words gently and felt at peace even though every eye in the room was looking at me. Of course, I've been waiting for the day when I could talk back to these mean girls, but I've always imagined yelling my head off, telling them they are worthless fools. But they're not worthless fools. They have just made some bad decisions, like I have.

I thought, even as I was speaking, that the girl would reach out and slug me. Or at least get her friends to laugh at me again. But she didn't. She broke down in sobs, still holding on to my hand, and slumped into her seat. She wouldn't let go of my hands. I thought, Only a Latin girl would do this! The other girls didn't know what to do either, and some of them began to cry. It felt like I was starring in a bad movie.

Finally she stood up again and gave me a kiss on each cheek. She said she was sorry and asked if I would forgive her. At that point I was so overwhelmed I just wanted to get away. I couldn't imagine staying in that room for another minute. I said, of course I had already forgiven her and walked out the door.

One of the teachers caught me by the arm as I headed for the main gate of the school. "Estas bien?" she asked, looking deep into my eyes. "I'm fine," I whispered, and with her permission I left school and walked home.

The girls at school have been much nicer to me since then. The boys are another thing. It's like I have a whole troop of bodyguards now who watch my every move and wait on me hand and foot. I've become something for them to fight for, and I have heard more than one of them say how they failed to make me feel safe. I don't think I will ever fit in at that school.

My parents are talking about sending me to the American school for my last year, so I'm trying to raise my grades and make sure I'm caught up.

Speaking of which, I've got tons of homework! Gotta go.

Love,
Gretchen

P.S. Karen is still crazy over Modesto. It doesn't matter to her that he's 18 and she's just 14, and they're from entirely different worlds. She talks about him every waking moment! He's coming to town again in a couple of weeks, and my parents have invited him for dinner. It will be amazing if Karen doesn't snap before then.

April 1
Pacific Palisades, California

Dear Gretchen,

I quit the tennis team yesterday and decided to go back to gymnastics. I want to win Nationals and RULE THE WORLD!

APRIL FOOL!

That's about as far from the truth as I could dream up. I'm still on the tennis team, but I haven't won a match yet. I am getting a little better with each practice, but I don't suppose I'll ever be seen at Wimbledon!

School is going well for me, but I had no idea how horrible it was for you! I am so proud that you could speak gently to those girls after they had said such terrible things right to your face. I think somehow they must have felt threatened by you. Anyway, it's wonderful to know that school is less stressful for you now. I'm sure you'll catch up in a hurry.

Things with Steve are going great! "Will you go steady with me, Mia?" He actually said that! Isn't that what our grandparents did, went steady? I said yes, of course, and so we're not just going out, we're going steady.

I'm not sure how to explain our relationship. I think of it as a "big" relationship, because we talk about big things, not the everyday stuff. Sometimes I look at him and feel amazed at the change in his life. And it's not like he's trying to be good or wise. Instead, it's like he just flipped a switch. And I feel the same way about my life—as if God is growing us up together.

Steve and I are in chapter 3 of Proverbs, and last week we found this piece of advice amazing!

> Don't be impressed with your own wisdom. Instead, fear the Lord and turn your back on evil. Then you will gain renewed health and vitality. Proverbs 3:7-8

At first I laughed because I could use some renewed health and vitality! What really struck me about these verses is the turning-away-from-evil part. Talking about others in a mean way. Drinking. Cheating. Lying. . . . All of those things that are so easy to do in high school.

Steve really took these verses to heart and must have read them so many times that they're now embedded in his brain. He says that before the accident he didn't fear God as much as he feared his friends. He wanted to be liked by everyone so much that he was willing to do things and say things that probably hurt God—and hurt himself.

For me, I think the first verse is the easiest one to pass over, but maybe the hardest to do. "Don't be impressed with your own wisdom." Don't think you're smarter than everyone else. Don't think your opinion is the only one that matters. That's tough. I think it's easy not to drink. But it's hard not to think that I'm better or wiser than the kids who are drinking. I'm going to have to work on that!

Steve is good for me. I don't know what falling in love is all about, but I must be coming close to the edge. I wonder if the same thing is happening to him.

Carol and I have been spending a lot of time together lately. We go running when we can, usually up to the waterfall above Temescal, and I have offered to help her with the fifth-grade kids at church. She is a big sister to one of the girls, and I think I might apply at the Sister-to-Sister Agency too.

I slept over at Carol's house last Saturday, but I didn't travel the usual way to end up at her front door! My dad, Johnny, Charlie, and I went fishing up the coast in the morning. I wanted to fish and go to Carol's house, but there was no way to do both because the guys weren't coming home until late. So my dad came up with a plan. "Why don't you just swim ashore? She lives right at Big Rock, and we can pass that way around lunchtime." It sounded like a great adventure, so I called Carol and asked her if she would paddle a surfboard halfway out to meet me.

We fished all morning and caught enough halibut and sea bass for a few family barbecues. At 11:30 we headed the boat toward Carol's house, which was easy to find from the water because of the new paint color her mom picked out this year: pink! I had my bathing suit on and my toothbrush and a change of clothes wrapped in plastic bags strapped across my back. We floated in front of her house for a while, but we didn't see Carol right away, so Johnny threw in a line.

I love the ocean just like you do and have been swimming, fishing, and exploring it since I was in diapers. But there are a few things that still give me the creeps. Stingrays, for one. Jellyfish, for another, though I've never been stung . . . and of course, sharks.

Well, here I am, ready to dive into the deep blue when Johnny hauls in a four-foot, wiggling soup shark. It had everything a normal shark would have: fins, tail, gills. It squirmed its way off the line as Johnny pulled it out of the water. It swam near the surface for a moment, looking at me, watching me, so he could tell "the others" which leg of mine looked meatier.

I stood on the platform at the back of the boat and all I could think of was that shark swimming below, just waiting for me. I knew he was harmless—at least in my head I knew it. Goodness, they don't even have teeth, but I kept thinking, Where there's one, there's more! My dad and brothers were doubled over in hysterics as I hesitated.

Finally, I dove into the water and swam like a speedboat to Carol, who was now waiting on her surfboard. I could've won the Olympics the way I tore through that water. Carol met me 30 yards from shore. I didn't mention anything about her feet being chewed on until we were up on the beach waving good-bye to the boat.

I sure love the ocean, but between being rescued by the lifeguard, capsizing the Hobie, and swimming with the sharks, I'm about ready to give up and enjoy it from my beach chair.

Carol and I talk about you all the time, wishing you were here and still hoping that you will come back soon to visit.

Which reminds me! Yes, you are definitely, officially, personally invited to come and stay with us this summer! It's not a joke, not make-believe. I have it all figured out. You can have my room, and I will move upstairs to the back attic room, where I love to listen to the rain (which we never get . . . but that's not the point). So ask your parents and let's start making plans!

On that note, I say adios. My dad is taking us out for ice cream! Better go!

Love,
Mia

April 6
Quito, Ecuador

★ ★ ★

Dear Mia,

Karen has lost it! She is so in love with Stella's brother that she can't eat, can't do her schoolwork, and talks about him in her sleep. He came for dinner a few nights ago, and boy was that an interesting evening! By the way, I loved your story about the sharks. I can see your brothers laughing hysterically as you dove in.

Back to Karen. When the doorbell rang, she was in front of the mirror pinching her cheeks for the hundredth time. She wore her hair in a long blonde braid down her back, just like an Indian girl would. I thought she would race down to see him as soon as he was let in, but instead she melted into a heap on her bed, sobbing unbelievable tears. She caught me off guard, but I guess she just couldn't handle the emotion of finally seeing Modesto again.

"So handsome . . . too far away . . . such big . . . kind eyes . . . not like them . . ." That's about all I could get out of her as she cried in my arms. I felt sorry for her. She is a sweet girl, but she is fighting a losing battle, falling in love with someone who lives in such a different world.

My parents and Stella greeted Modesto at the door. I ran down as soon as I could, leaving poor Karen to rub the red out of her eyes by herself. I will admit again that Modesto is incredibly handsome. His dark blue poncho and white cotton shirt make him look like a warrior in disguise. I just hope Karen doesn't get too hurt by hoping for something that is impossible. I ought to know, from my experience with Matthew.

Juana had cooked all day so Stella wouldn't have to work while Modesto was there. My mom and I served the meal, and unlike Stella, I think Modesto feels at home anywhere. He and my dad hit it off right away, and time flew by that evening.

Mostly they talked about how Modesto has been coming to town to try and get help from the government for his irrigation project. He explained how so many of the Indians have moved to the slums of the city, looking for work but have found only poverty instead. Modesto doesn't just want to fix one irrigation canal for himself or his neighbors, but he wants to get people excited all over the country about moving back to the land where they can live healthier lives. "And water," he said, "is the key."

I haven't seen my dad so excited about something in years. He asked a million questions and pulled out a dozen maps. He kept Modesto there much longer than he should have, and poor Karen went to bed, leaving the two men still talking in Dad's study. I had to go to bed too and woke up in the morning to find Stella and Modesto in the kitchen together. My dad must have invited him to stay. Can you imagine Karen's eyes when she walked in to have breakfast and found Modesto at the table?!

As you can see, Karen's life is much more exciting than mine. Except for the fact that you have invited me to come and stay with you for the summer. My parents haven't given me any hope that I will be allowed to come, but that doesn't mean I won't still hope.

I'm nervous about switching schools. I haven't told you yet, but I have an interview this month at the American school. You can't just sign up. You have to write an essay about "An Experience That Changed Your Life," and then there is an interview with both a teacher and one of the administrators. I wrote the essay already, about visiting Stella's house, but I'm beyond nervous about the interview. Pray that I won't say anything stupid, bite my fingernails, or trip as I walk in the door. I would love to switch schools. Quite a few of the more normal kids at church go to this one.

Well, I'm beat. My brain is freezing up, and all I can do is imagine you swimming furiously with a shark at your heels. I miss you.

Remember, send me more news about Steve. I love hearing about how you're studying the Bible together while going steady. . . .

Love,
Gretchen

Dear Gretchen,

I never thought I would find myself on Crenshaw Boulevard, right in the heart of Los Angeles. My grandpa tells me stories about how he once rode a horse from the Palisades to a dairy farm near Hollywood. The roads were dirt, the freeways didn't exist, and yes, they used to milk cows in Hollywood!

Mikela is my new "little sister" and I have pledged to spend time with her once every two weeks. She lives a block off Crenshaw Boulevard, the ugliest place in the world. How is it that I have lived my whole life here and have never been more than five miles from the beach? I didn't even know such a gross place existed until I sat on the freeway forever to go 15 miles through the smog to Mikela's house.

She's only nine years old and in the third grade. She's really bright and way ahead of the other kids in school, but she has a tough home life. They told me at the Sister-to-Sister place that she needs someone to have fun with, someone who will play with her, and just be interested in her. I don't know why or how she has been so neglected, but I'm going to do all I can to be a great friend for her.

The first day, Mikela and I went out for ice cream. You should have seen her face as she licked her way through two scoops of double chocolate fudge. It was worth it to watch her enjoy the cone from start to finish. And she must have thanked me three times as we drove back to her house. It was hard to leave her there though, in the smog and the yuck of the city. I wanted to take her home with me.

Things with Steve are really going well. We spend lots of time together and I feel so boosted, so encouraged by him. His family has accepted me as another daughter. In fact, they always save the same chair for me at their dinner table. And the same goes for him at my house. I've never felt so free with a boy—free to believe what I believe and free to be who I am.

But here's the important question . . . WHY HASN'T HE KISSED ME YET? I'm afraid to ask him, because I don't want to rock this great boat we're in, but I like him more than just a brother. We've talked on the phone a hundred times, and still when I hear my mom yell, "Mia, Steve's on the phone . . ." I get butterflies. I guess we are going steady, and steady is the right word because we're just sitting in the same place—no moves forward, no moves backward.

Don't get me wrong—I'm not depressed. But I am confused and want so much more. With Johnny and Charlie the Tuna to look after me, I don't need another brother!

Good grief. Another letter that just babbles on. I miss you. Tell Karen that Charlie is in deep despair that she has found another boyfriend! (She'll know better than to believe that!)

And what about Matthew? Have you seen him at all? What has that been like? Just curious.

Love,
Mia

★ ★ ★

Dear Mia,

I have had so much homework! My application to the American school has been accepted on the condition that I get certain grades this year. I have less than one month to make up five months' worth of work, but I am determined to make it happen! I have never worked this hard at anything, EVER! So this letter will have to be short, even though I want to spend the next four hours with you instead of with an algebra book.

My Dad, Modesto, Matthew, and Mr. Montrane. It's the title of my new family soap opera. It's on channel 4 and airs every Saturday night. At least it did last Saturday.

Modesto was in town again, and my dad made sure he stopped by our house before he drove back to his village. Karen was in heaven. But again, it was all business and she only got to be with him for a few minutes. She doesn't hide the fact that she likes him, and I'm not sure what Modesto thinks, except he is always very polite to her.

The doorbell rang and I answered it. Kind of. Wasn't I surprised when I peeped through the hole to find a grinning Matthew and Mr. Montrane peering back at me in the round glass? I almost didn't open it for them. My dad noticed that I was staring at the door and yelled, "Gretchen, could you get that please?" I thought, Here goes nothing . . . or something!

My dad invited Mr. Montrane over to talk with Modesto and to ask for money or contacts for his irrigation project. I didn't listen in on their talk, but that's my best guess. Knowing Mr. Montrane, he'll give Modesto all he needs and more. I really like that man. Why can't Matthew be more like him?

Matthew, on the other hand, was sitting in my dad's study for what? Just to make me squirm in my own house? To see if I was ready to be involved in any more of his little projects? I don't know why he was there. But I can tell you this for sure: I couldn't wait for him to be chauffeured back to his hacienda. I sat in my room, looking out my balcony—and I wasn't going to tell you this part—but I cried and cried, and wished I had never met him.

That's pretty depressing stuff, but I really only had that one night to be depressed again. I've been writing and memorizing and studying so hard, there is no time to be depressed. Oh, and Mikela sounds like a real sweetie. Tell her I hope to meet her too if I get to visit this summer.

I promise I'll write sooner next time I hear from you. Until then.

Much love,
Gretchen

P.S. Tell Steve that I say, "What are you waiting for? Just kiss the girl!"

May 10
Pacific Palisades, California

Hi, Gretchen,

You remembered my birthday! I got the present the day before your last letter came, and you are soooooooo sweet. Thank you for the beautiful sweater. Alpaca wool costs a fortune over here and the quality is never that good. Of course, my mom inspected the wool with a microscope, and she is very jealous!

The ring is perfect. I spin it around on my finger and look at the incredible detail of it. It's such a great reminder of how friends can still be friends even though they live in different hemispheres. Thank you!

I showed off the ring Wednesday night when my family and Steve's met for dinner at the beach club. I passed it around the table and told them the story of how if I ever needed to hold your hand, I just reach across the moon to find it. They sure hope you will come to visit this summer. Robin, Steve's little sister, is an animal fanatic and she started talking about all the animals that live in the rain forests of South America. She asked, "Will Gretchen be able to tell me about the howler monkeys? Mia, has she seen any emerald tree boas?"

It was a nice evening, and we stayed longer than usual, because it's finally staying light past six o'clock. A crowd had gathered down at the volley-ball court, so after Robin's questions subsided a bit, Steve and I followed the loud cheers and went down to find Sanchez and Marco playing two guys from Samohi. Each team had won a game, and they were in the middle of the third when we walked up. The guys were flying all over the court, kicking up sand and making great plays.

Just as Marco said, "14 to 13," Steve got this goofy grin on his face and pulled me away from the game. "I want to see who wins . . . ," I said as he tugged on my arm. When I turned to look at him, I could see the mischief in his eyes. We ran down near the water and sat in between two of the Hobies that were beached by the fence.

He asked first. "Mia, may I kiss you?" And believe me it didn't take me long to say yes. I was ready. "Ah, that felt good," he said. "I've been wanting to kiss you for a long time, but I've resisted. I want this relationship to be different, to be special every day." I punched him on the shoulder and said he didn't have to wait quite that long next time! We sat and talked for a bit, forgotting about the volleyball game. Later I found out that the guys from Samohi won, so it was definitely worth it to go and kiss instead!

Thanks again for the awesome birthday presents. I am so lucky to have a friend like you!

Love,
Mia

May 17
Quito, Ecuador

★ ★ ★

Dear Mia,

I am so glad you like your birthday presents. I wish I could have given them to you in person.

To tell you the truth, I was worried about the ring I sent you, because I designed it myself. Our cook, Juana, has a brother who makes silver jewelry. I asked her about a necklace she was wearing once, and she said her brother can make anything out of silver.

One day in school, while I was eating lunch, I got this flash that I wanted to make you something for your birthday. Once that thought was in my head, I couldn't think of doing anything else, and finally I came up with the ring idea. In my English class (I'm breezing through that one!) I made a sketch of two girls holding hands over the moon. It was a horrible, little stick-figure drawing, but it seemed perfect for you and me. I brought the sketch home and showed it to Juana, and for once she didn't chase me out of the kitchen.

Juana's brother made two rings: one for me and one for

you. If you look on the inside of the ring, you will see that he wrote our names on the figures in tiny print. I didn't believe the names were even there until Juana pulled her eyeglasses close to magnify the writing. I love my ring. I'm so glad you like yours.

I'm counting the days until school is out. So far, we have one summer vacation planned, and that is a trip to Chile. There is an area called Valparaiso along the coast of Chile that has been called the Garden of Eden. They say you can grow anything there and that the landscape takes your breath away. It sounds better than heading into the jungle again, but I'm still hoping for a trip north, not a trip south. I won't bother my parents though. They know how much I want to visit you, and I'm trying to be patient and hope for the best.

Sorry I can't write more. So much to read and so little time!

Love,
Gretchen

Dear Mia,

I just want to tuck this little note in with my letter before I send it off to you. My parents called me into their room last night after getting a phone call from the States. They had just talked to your mom, who wanted to personally invite me to come and stay for the summer. "Do you really want to go?" they asked me. "You've never been away from the family for such a long time, but we're leaving it up to you."

I had never expected to make the decision myself, and that threw me for a loop. But it didn't throw me for very long. I'm coming to stay with you this summer. All we have to do now is set the date! Yippee! Write soon.

Love,
Gretchen

Dear Gretchen,

I'm so excited you're coming to stay!!!!! I'm going to take the room upstairs, and you get mine. Everyone can't wait to see you, including all the kids at church, because I couldn't keep my mouth shut. Steve kept saying, "No way, she's really coming? No way! That's awesome!"

Mikela and I have been spending a lot of time together, more than the required once every other week. I'm getting used to driving the freeway, but I know I'll never like it.

Yesterday I taught her how to do a handstand and a backbend on her living-room floor. She's pretty good! And limber! She wants me to keep teaching her more tricks, so I promised I would come once a week and we could have a mini-gymnastics class. Now she's begging her mom for a leotard! I'll have to dig her up an old one of mine.

I can't wait till you meet her, Gretchen. She really is special.

The only other news is that Nationals are this weekend, and no one from my gym is going. My coach called and asked if I wanted to know the results once he heard, and I said . . . yes. God may have closed that door for me, but I can't say I don't want to keep peeking back through the cracks.

School is out for me on June 20, but you can come sooner if you want. As long as you don't go to the beach every day while I'm studying for finals! That would drive me crazy! But if you sit quietly in the living room reading science books, I'll be just fine.

Well, writing you has become such a big part of my life that I'm not sure what will happen to me when you're here. Maybe I'll start writing in a journal, or maybe I'll just keep writing you, but I'll fold the letters into paper airplanes and fly them onto your bed.

I should be called Miss Babble. How many times this year have I wasted space and had to add extra stamps to your letters just because I write about nothing?

In an effort to save space, I'm going to say good-bye. <u>Adios!</u>

Love,
Mia

June 2
Quito, Ecuador

★ ★ ★

<u>Hola,</u> Mia,

School is over. What a relief! Yesterday my parents told me that I <u>barely</u> made it into the American school. It was so close that a counselor called and spoke with the principal of my current school. They wanted to verify my records. It must have looked odd having F's and A's all on the same report card. Thank goodness I was able to learn enough Spanish in time to catch up in my classes. That's a heavy load off my back.

Moving on . . .

Matthew. I was hoping I would never have to write his name again. But here he is, sneaking his way back into my letters.

Modesto is changing so many people's lives. Karen, of course, will never be the same because of her smothering devotion to him. My dad loves him too and has spent hours and hours calling politicians, writing letters, speaking with every sort of agency that exists, and who knows what else for him. Mr. Montrane is doing the same, but he has so much more pull in this country and money to back up his words. Matthew seems intrigued by it all, and according to what he told me, he is a "new man!" Whatever. All I know is that our house has become a meeting place for big, crazy ideas, and all of this is because of Modesto and his simple thoughts about water.

"I must speak with you!" Matthew said the other night when he and his father came over again to talk business with Modesto. I know I rolled my eyes at him, but he looked serious, not like the Matthew I'm used to. I said no. Right there where everyone could see if they wanted to, he got down on his knees and said, "Please, I must speak with you. I cannot go another minute with this pain burning in my heart." Oh, brother. Mr. Dramatic. He should be in movies.

Thank goodness Elsie and Susanna weren't in the room, because I'm sure they would have started giggling, but only my mom noticed that Matthew was begging at my knees. She said, "Why don't the two of you have some lemonade out in the courtyard." Thanks, Mom.

Once we were in the courtyard I told him I didn't want to hear what he had to say. He laughed that beautiful laugh of his, and it almost killed me, because I love that laugh. I said he better make it quick because I had better things to do. Even though I had nothing else to do, doing nothing was better than talking to him.

He said he broke up with his girlfriend. He said he has been having a hard time at school. He said he can't sleep, eat, or ride his horse. And he said it is all because of me. "You changed me," he said. "You opened my eyes. You have made me a new man."

Man? I struggled to listen to him. When I think of a man, I think of my father, your father, his father. Could he ever be like one of them? A compassionate, honest man? A godly man who thinks of others first? I listened to him speak, and the more he talked, the more the old feelings came back. I found myself being swayed by his eyes . . . those eyes!

The really hard part was when he said, "Will you forgive me?" I had never thought that someday I would have to forgive him for being so cruel to me. I didn't say anything for a long time, and I remember looking away, hoping he might disappear. I couldn't say yes. I couldn't. So I didn't.

I walked back inside the house and left him sitting there.

I went to my room, cleaned up, and went to bed. Ever since then I have been trying so hard not to think about him that I swear I must think about him more than I ever have. I can't forgive him. He used me, he hurt me, and he made me feel like a toy—something to be had, something to be owned. Ugh.

Don't tell me that I should forgive him, because I already know I should. I know it's the right thing to do. Forgiving those girls at school, girls that I hardly knew or ever really wanted to know, was easier. Forgiving Matthew is different, because I feel like all of the terrible thoughts I have about him, all of the mad thoughts, somehow protect me from getting more hurt. I feel sick just thinking about it.

Nice way to end a letter, huh? So many great things are happening in my life besides Matthew, so I'll say good-bye, knowing that we're going to have a whole, awesome summer together! By the way, my mom said I could call you this week to work out all the details of my coming. Talk to you soon!

Love,
Gretchen

June 10
Pacific Palisades, California

Dear Gretchen,

It was so fun to talk to you on the phone. I haven't heard your voice in a year, and you sounded different. You have a Spanish accent! That was funny, but you are still you. It felt so good to talk, didn't it?

It has been a wild and crazy year for you and for me, so just think what fun we'll have over the summer. We don't even need any new memories. . . . We've built up enough stuff to talk about for years.

Mikela is great and she's shaping up to be a good little gymnast. Sometimes I think I'm learning more from her than she is learning from me! I can't wait to introduce you two when you come.

PLEASE bring some pictures of Ecuador and your family. Everyone is going crazy that you're coming back, and they want to see proof of you actually chopping your way through the jungle and wading through piranha-filled rivers. The kids at church have asked me so many questions about what you'll be doing this summer that I should sign a contract with you and be your agent!

I can't wait to see you walk off that plane. And you better not give me that silly grin of yours. I want a huge smile and NO TEARS. You always cry about everything, and this time you'd better not! Or I'll be right there crying with you!

This is it. The last letter. I figure with the way Ecuadorian mail works, I better play it safe.

See you soon!

Love,
Mia

June 16
Quito, Ecuador

* * *

Dear Mia,

Unbelievable. I just got your last letter and, for sure, this will be mine. Otherwise anything after today will arrive at your house after I'm already there. No use in writing stuff down that I can tell you in person. And there are six more days before I leave, so there will be plenty of new things to tell you.

I was sleeping in my beautifully carved bed and just happened to be wearing my "flowing nightgown" that you sent me. It was early in the morning before the sun rose, and I woke up suddenly because there was a strange noise in my room. I sat there, confused for a while, and then I heard it again, a click against the shutters. Then another, and another. At first I thought it was a woodpecker trying to drill into my room. Karen woke up and asked, "What is that?" That's when I decided to open the shutters and look outside.

I opened them slowly to peek out, and there was

Matthew standing in the courtyard with a handful of stones. I was so surprised that I laughed, and of course Karen jumped up to see what I was laughing at. We stood there for a long time, and the more we laughed the more Matthew grinned. What a spectacle! Soon all the other shutters were opening around the house, and the whole family was gazing down at him. But did he mind? No, he loved it. Nothing fazes Matthew.

With everyone staring down at him, he swung his guitar from around his back and started to sing a Spanish folk song that I've heard many times. I was embarrassed. I was amazed. What nerve he has! I listened from my balcony and applauded with the others when he was done. Then he asked, very quietly and in Spanish, if I would come down and join him for a cup of sunrise coffee.

There I was, in my Juliet nightgown, being serenaded by the one I used to think would be my Romeo. And now he wanted me to forgive him. The song must have softened me, or maybe I was still asleep, because when I went to bed the night before I was still set on not giving him any leeway . . . I could still hear him say, loud and clear, "You are so beautiful. How can I help myself?"

I dressed and went down for coffee. He admitted that he

had hurt me and that he was sorry. This time, I began to believe him. A little. And I did forgive him. I said I would as long as he promised to have more respect for women. And I meant it.

I also made him take a sacred oath. With his right hand on the Bible and the other hand pressed against his heart he said, "I, Matthew Montrane, will never kiss a girl again" (then he said, "wait a minute," but I glared at him and made him keep going) ". . . will never kiss a girl again . . . who is not my girlfriend. I, Matthew Montrane, will respect ALL women . . . and not treat them like things to be had."

I thought that was enough. Once we got going, he repeated the words like he was announcing new ideas to the world.

Boys! I thought I had them all figured out, and then comes Matthew. From the beginning I've never quite known what to expect from him. I can't believe I'm saying this, but watching him be so sincere and apologetic, I felt sorry for him. There must be some good behind those handsome eyes for him to make such a big deal about being forgiven.

Well, no point in talking about him now. I'll have the whole summer to tell you about him or forget about him, which would probably be better. I've certainly learned a lot this year. But the best news is that I'm ready to get on that plane and have the best summer ever, with you, my best friend.

Mucho, mucho,
mucho amor,
Gretchen

Facts about Ecuador

- Ecuador is a small country in South America (not in Africa!). More than 10 million people live there, most of whom live along the coast or in the highlands. Very few people live deep in the rain forest, which is known as El Oriente or La Selva.

- The name *Ecuador* is the Spanish word for *equator*. Look at a map and see how the imaginary line of the equator runs right through Ecuador. Because the sun hits the earth most directly at the equator, all of the world's tropical rain forests are found along the equator, including the rain forests of Ecuador.

- People have been living in Ecuador for thousands of years. Over time, many of the separate Indian cultures developed sophisticated tools that they used for farming, hunting, and building.

- The Incas were a powerful group of Indians who conquered much of South America in the 14th and 15th centuries. They were ruled by the Inca sun god who passed on his throne to his heirs. In the Inca world there were armies and generals, but also a complex system of irrigated farmland that supported each community with food, clothes, and housing. The communities were linked by a stone highway that ran the length of South America. The Incas are well known for their spectacular feats in construction and engineering.

- Francisco Pizarro, a Spaniard, landed in South America in 1531. Driven by his hunger for gold, Pizarro and his 168 men and 27 horses began a siege on the Incas that had lasting effects. The Inca Empire collapsed, and the Spaniards looted, murdered, and burned everything in their way, always looking for more gold and riches. Many of the people of Ecuador were made slaves and sent to work in mines to find the gold Pizarro so desperately wanted.

- Simón Bolívar is a well-known name in Ecuador. He was the man who, with his troops and commanders, liberated Ecuador and other South American countries from Spanish rule in the 1880s. Ever since gaining its independence from Spain, Ecuador has had many rulers and many governments, but no revolutions.

- The Roman Catholic Church has done much to aid the native people of Ecuador. Though Pizarro and his men committed many atrocities in the name of religion, the Catholic church has sought to take care of the Indians. Just this century the church gave one-half million acres of land to native peoples.

- There are four geographical regions in Ecuador: the Oriente, the Costa, the Sierra, and the Galápagos Islands. These different regions house an *incredible* abundance of plants and animals. There are 320 types of mammals, more than 1,550 species of birds, and 20,000 plant species, not to mention reptiles, insects (millions of them), and fish living within the country's borders. Many of these animals and plants are *endemic* to Ecuador, meaning they can be found only in Ecuador and nowhere else.

- The Andes Mountains of South America are a very visible feature in the landscape of Ecuador. The mountains run north to south the entire length of the country. Up and down the mountain range is a line of snow-covered volcanoes reaching to the sky. Along the range, the volcanoes named Iliniza, Sangay, and Altar have summits that reach above 17,000 feet. Cotopaxi, Antisana, and Cayambe are all more than 19,000 feet. Chimborazo is Ecuador's most impressive volcano standing at 20,823 feet.

- Quito is the capital of Ecuador. Almost one and a half million people live there. The city sits far above sea level at 9,405 feet. The weather is so nice, some people say it's like "eternal spring."

When Jane G. Meyer's best friend moved overseas with her missionary family, so began a three-year exchange of heartfelt letters that whizzed back and forth across the oceans. Each day was a race to the mailbox as the two 15-year-old girls recounted their troubles and joys to one another. Years later, after Jane sifted through an old box of memories and found her bundle of blue-and-white airmail envelopes, the idea for writing *Hands Across the Moon* was born.

Jane now lives in Santa Barbara, California, with her husband, Douglas and their two children, Andrew and Madeleine. She still writes letters the old-fashioned way—in a quiet space with ink pens and paper—and encourages you to write to your friends too.

thirsty(?)™

Sammy's gone.

I would have stopped him . . .

A sneak peek at

Kyra's Story

by Dandi Daley Mackall

They killed Sammy. Maybe we all did.

He's dead. He died.

Don't you dare—not any of you—try saying my brother is *gone,* that he *passed, passed away, passed over,* had a terrible *accident.*

Sammy was 17. Now he's dead. Just like that.

Dylan says Sammy is in heaven. But even that doesn't make him less dead . . . or us less guilty.

I'm sitting on a shiny, wooden bench outside the courtroom. Footsteps echo through the hall, people in a hurry, with places to go, people to go to. A door slams somewhere, and a burst of voices tangle and bounce against the cold, cement walls.

Above, to my right, a branch scrapes a high window. Rain blurs the windowpane—blown there hard, smacked to a stop and dropped, sliding down in sheets, like hands grasping but finding nothing to hold on to.

"I'm afraid it's going to be a while, Kyra." The assistant DA smiles at me like she's afraid I'll change my mind about testifying. She sets down her briefcase and gives me a we're-in-this-together nod. Just two girls here. But Sammy wasn't *her* twin. And she should know *she'd* back down before I would.

"I'm okay," I say.

"It's good to go over your testimony in your head if you want to, while you're waiting." She tugs at her thin, black ponytail and unbuttons her gray suit jacket. "Remember. Just answer the questions. You're going to do fine, Kyra." She picks up her briefcase and goes back into the courtroom.

I try to see inside but only get a glimpse of the guard at the door and part of a row of strangers in the back.

I've watched enough bad TV and *Law and Order* reruns to know you can't always trust judges and juries. They can't always trust the witnesses sworn in to tell the truth, the whole truth, and nothing but the truth. People shape their stories, their *truth,* to make themselves look better, to make the world a place they can live in without going crazy. I know that better than anybody.

So maybe people won't get what they deserve in this trial. Sammy sure didn't deserve what he got.

I stand up, pace down the hall, and glance both ways through the corridor. No Miranda. No Tyrone. I don't even know for sure if they'll show. I don't have any idea what they're going to say or who will believe them.

Maybe they won't believe me. Maybe nobody will. I can't blame them. For 17 years I didn't believe me either.

But believe *this.* Sammy James is dead. And somebody has to know how it happened, how we really got to this, a murder trial in Macon, Iowa, the first in our town's history.

So I might as well write it all down—I won't leave anything out. I'll tell it just like it happened. It all started New Year's Day, when Mitchell Wade sauntered into town like a New Year's resolution somebody forgot to make, a resolution that from that moment on, changed life as we knew it.

degrees OF GUILT

A sneak peek at

Miranda's Story

by Melody Carlson

I'm going down, I think as I ride to the police station in the back of the cop car. Miranda Maria Sanchez is going down. And I don't even care. I guess I know it's what I deserve. There's some satisfaction in knowing this. Imagining myself behind bars helps to take my mind off Sammy. I try not to think about him. Or the fact that he died in my living room. Last night. Right there on the ugly purple sofa.

Sammy, where are you?

I know I should rest, but I can't go to sleep. Or maybe I am asleep and this is all just a hideous nightmare and I will wake up and everything will be back to what it used to be. And I'll live differently, make better choices, and Sammy will still be alive. But I know I'm not asleep and the wail of last night's sirens still rings in my ears and the flashing emergency lights are scorched into my brain like a hot sizzling brand that will burn there forever. But what's worse—and it makes me ache to remember—is how Sammy looked before they wheeled him away.

I never thought the first dead person I'd see would

be one of my oldest and dearest friends. Or that I'd be the cause of his death. At first I thought he was just asleep. Okay, maybe passed out even. And that in itself didn't seem so surprising since I'd never seen Sammy drink anything more than a single beer in his entire life, and that was last New Year's, back when life was still normal. Even then *I* had been the one to talk him into it.

But for some reason Sammy really cut loose last night. At first I was pretty shocked that he even came over at all. I mean, Sammy has never been into partying. But he was definitely the life of the party for a short while. Totally unSammylike. And even though I was pretty wasted myself, I remember thinking, *How weird is that?* But then stupidly I said nothing, did nothing. Just kept on partying like I'd done over the last few months.

Now I close my eyes and feel my front teeth bite into my lower lip. Hard. I taste the blood—salty warm. And I just sit here, saying nothing. I cannot believe this is really happening. Maybe it's not. Perhaps if I wait long enough, I'll open my eyes and be someplace else, like Mitch's English class. Daydreaming again. My favorite one—about how he and I will run away together shortly after I graduate. We'll drive away in his silver Porsche and everything will be fine.

Then I hear someone clearing a throat and I look up. It's Detective Sanders, and I'm at the police station.

This is not going to go away.

Sammy's gone.

I could have stopped him . . .

A sneak peek at

Tyrone's Story

by Sigmund Brouwer

Whatever anyone tells you about Sammy and the night he died, it's a lie. Because I know the truth.

Not that I'm going to tell the cops.

Maybe half an hour ago I was sitting in a math class, contemplating a theory about life that essentially says it's a highway and too many of us become roadkill because we're too dumb to realize what's behind the bright lights that mesmerize us. Then that prissy old secretary from the principal's office knocked on the door and handed my teacher, Mr. Gimble, a note.

Gimble adjusted his bifocals and strained to read the note, then said that Tyrone Larson was requested at the office.

I wasn't worried it was something like the day Amy Sing went down and was told her old man had just suffered a heart attack, because, frankly, my old man doesn't exist for me. I figured a heart attack would make him the first roadkill that made sense in my life. Instead, I was worried, for good reason, that it was about Sammy. Sammy just did the roadkill thing, stepping out into the bright lights of a party. It's all anybody can talk about at Macon High.

Sure enough, there was a cop waiting for me at the office—some guy with a big belly I recognized because he sets up speed traps and lets the businessmen who can afford the tickets whiz by while he waits to nab all the teenage drivers desperately escaping our prison after the final buzzer of the school day.

Now the cop speaks to me in a low sympathetic voice that he probably thinks is going to fool me. "We need you for some routine questions," he says.

"Routine questions?" I ask. "I guess that means you're looking for routine answers. How much use could that be for anyone?"

He stares at me. "I had it in my mind we were going to speak someplace privately here in the school. But now I think I'll take you down to the station."

"Let me call a lawyer," I say. I should be afraid. But I turn the fear into a wave of anger. It feels good to surf it. So I pull my cell phone out of my pocket and start punching numbers, like I know exactly who to call.

The cop doesn't say a word. Just pushes me out the door as I put the phone to my ear to pick up the latest sports news on this service I subscribe to. He escorts me to his police car in the parking lot.

With all the kids in my math class staring out the window and watching me get inside the backseat.

Then I go.

thirsty(?)™

www.thirstybooks.com